TO Kay
FROM tim onstad

ONSTAD MYTHOLOGY

World of Legends

MAGIC AND SCIENCE COME TOGETHER IN WAYS NEVER BEFORE SEEN

by

Tim Onstad

DORRANCE
PUBLISHING CO
EST. 1920
PITTSBURGH, PENNSYLVANIA 15238

The contents of this work, including, but not limited to, the accuracy of events, people, and places depicted; opinions expressed; permission to use previously published materials included; and any advice given or actions advocated are solely the responsibility of the author, who assumes all liability for said work and indemnifies the publisher against any claims stemming from publication of the work.

Dorrance Publishing Co
585 Alpha Drive
Suite 103
Pittsburgh, PA 15238
Visit our website at *www.dorrancebookstore.com*

ISBN: 978-1-6853-7185-2
eISBN: 978-1-6853-7727-4

Onstad Mythology

World of Legends

Magic and science come together in ways never before seen

CONTENTS

PROLOGUE

Stories have been told for as long as there have been words to tell them. Well over five-hundred thousand years ago, the first stories could very well be responsible for civilization itself. The furred storyteller gave the group a sense of escape and a sense of belonging, even inventing common rituals, morals, and ideals based on these stories. Entire families of hominid would become enchanted and enraptured by the thought of tree bark glowing as blue as the sky and an elder's youthful fur coat growing back in full.

Though they would've thought that their bodies were healed by the Shaman's words and strange rites, what was really being healed was their soul and peace of mind. Now, there was security in a world full of horrifying monsters and chaotic universe ending events. What was once wildlife became sapient life with shared goals and hierarchies. If not inspired by simple stories and magic rites, then something must've gotten them to do such laborious and time-consuming feats such as making a sun small enough to live on the ground.

If that sounds farfetched, then consider this: All over world, millions, if not billions, of dollars are spent every year to create or recreate an experience unlike one's own life, whether it's through inventions derived from sci-fi or theme parks derived from flights of fancy. In the information age, stories come in more forms than ever before, ranging from video games to movies to cartoons.

Everyone wants to escape into something beyond themselves and their circle of perception. Whether we're *geek* or *chic*, we've all been touched and moved by a great story at some point in our lives. Beit ancient religious epics or modern superhero blockbusters, it has shaped culture and what we aspire to achieve in life. Which is why it's such a shame that these incredible portals of escape for the young and old have been corrupted by ever so human flaws of conformity and self-preservation.

I started writing *Onstad Mythology* to usher in a period of optimism and unity in a world that is so horrifically divided. All too often, people with a staggering amount of power & influence over culture tell us to focus on our differences and how they make us evil. Even though we don't all have the same life experience, we humans do share the incredible ability to imagine and empathize.

Some of us prefer to empathize with a slice of life drama meant to project one's own triumphs and shortcomings onto, while others prefer fantastic tales of long-eared magical people and tusked, warmongering people to make one's deepest dreams come true. What I've done is simple: apply our wonderful world of legends to the current day and age for the first time in centuries.

1
SOLAR WAR

Eleven-thousand years ago, in what would now be the province of Skåne in the southern tip of Sweden, the area was completely covered in snow and glacial ice since the Earth was in the middle of an Ice Age. To the tribesmen, the great glacier was known as the Altura Mountains, as they resembled bluish white hills and peaks.

A party of white-haired, Elven huntsmen in mammoth fur pelts could be seen trekking the white and blue sloping wasteland with their ancient Neanderthal Shaman named Bergia. It was freezing cold, yet it was a clear day with a bright, blue sky while white rabbits could be seen racing round glacial hills and crevasses. The huntsman pulled back on his bow, eager for a hearty meal, only to have the rabbits go back into their icy burrow.

The Shaman, meanwhile, had his eyes tightly closed as his staff glowed a shade of light green. He carefully looked across the spiritual plane for the contained spirit of an elk when, suddenly, he perceived two souls that were incredibly bright auras that seemed to be in the exact outline of two Human women. His eyes went wide as he looked up at the midday sky where two shining, white rain drops seemingly came down from the Sun.

"Look at that!" exclaimed the Shaman, pointing at it.

"Woah," remarked one of the huntsmen, gazing up at the sky as the two shapes gradually separated from the Sun. "What are they?"

"Th-they're some kind of spirit," said Bergia, massaging his brow ridge "But in all my ages of practicing magic, I've never seen anything like it."

"Strange," said another huntsman. "It's not a bird or anything else like that. Should we go and check it out, Spirit Guide?"

Bergia brought his hand back to his side and said, "Sure, but keep your wits about you. It could be a new spell from the Wolf people, so follow me."

He soon led them across the ice and past crevasses until they laid eyes on a most incredible sight: Two women with skin as white as vanilla, their eyes blue and their hair blonde.

They descended from the heavens with a brilliant, white, angelic light glowing off their humble bodies. They appeared more powerful than all the creatures in nature as their very being radiated heat like flying bonfires. The huntsmen had their arrows at the ready with their bows fully bent back as the two ladies landed gracefully and gently on their feet while a patch of snow and ice melted away into a circular puddle of water.

The Shaman stepped forward towards them and knelt before the excellence of the two spirits.

"Salutations to you," he said. "What great Human familiars might you be?"

"We're better than Humans, mortal," said the lady in a soft, celestial voice. "We are goddesses. I'm Eostre, and this is my friend, Stjarna." Eostre motioned to Stjarna, who waved at them, winking.

"How do you do?" said Stjarna humbly

"Hey Spirit Guide," said one of the huntsmen, "should we still attack?"

Eostre chuckled at the idea.

"Even if you did, your weapons would be no good against me," she said. "As goddesses, we're immortal, transcended spiritual agents."

"Immortal spirit?" said one of the huntsmen as they all huddled closer. "You mean like our Spirit Guide, Bergia?"

"We're more than mere guides," bragged Eostre. "We control the universe, and there're whole tribes of us out in the cosmos."

"And she's the Goddess of Springtime; daughter of Sol herself," said Stjarna.

"Sol?" asked Bergia, pointing up at the Sun. "You came from the Sol?"

"Y-yes," smiled Stjarna. "We control the Sun, the seasons, and the weather, too. See how we're already melting the snow?" She pointed down to her feet where a sphere of glacial ice had been carved out, revealing unsightly greyish-brown topsoil underneath.

"Yeah, it's so hot now" said the huntsmen, taking off their pelts and fanning themselves. "Is this what you mean by season?"

"Y-yeah, just like how spices change the flavor of meat," explained Stjarna, "our seasons change the Earth's temperature and make grass & flowers grow from nothing."

"Grass and flowers," smiled Bergia. "Now that would be a sight!"

"We'll make the grass and the flowers spring into life from nothing," said Eostre, "on one condition."

"I've been a Shaman for 550,000 years," said Bergia. "Anything you want of us, I'll be more than happy to provide for you Goddesses."

"We need to season the Sun in order to trigger springtime," explained Eostre. "So as a special covenant, gather your finest juniper and burn it, so it goes to our realm, Alfheimr, so that we could use it to fuel the Sun."

"We could certainly do that, Goddess Eostre," said Bergia, bringing his hand out to be shaken. Eostre soon grabbed his hand and shook it as part of the agreement before Bergia yelled in pain, for Eostre's mere touch was burning his hand.

"Bergia!" exclaimed the huntsmen, running towards him. "Are you okay?"

He held up his charred hand to show first and second-degree burns, though the cold air numbed a lot of the pain.

"The Goddess burned me like fire!" he exclaimed while wincing in pain.

"I'm terribly sorry," said Eostre, chuckling nervously. "I'm too powerful for your world of Midgard. I mean, I'm meant to transcend nature, and I'm forbidden to be here for too long."

"So we best be off," said Stjarna as she floated up into midair getting, farther and farther away from the ground as Eostre soon followed.

"Alfheimr!" exclaimed Stjarna once they were high enough for the mortals not to hear "Midgard? You named a middle world and a heaven after those two dorks on the city authority!"

"They don't have to know," shrugged Eostre as they passed through a cloud. "They're only Hyaman, or whatever those mortals called themselves."

"Your mom is going to kill us!" said Stjarna fearfully. "Why did I ever think this was a good idea?"

"Hey," said Eostre, patting Stjarna on the back, "it was either create a covenant with mortals or allow my mother's stupid solar fireball to leave us in the dark!"

"I see now," sighed Stjarna remembering their plan. "But how are we going to change the seasons when our powers aren't even strong enough to tweak the Earth's orbit?"

"Who said anything about changing the seasons," smirked Eostre

"Uhh, you did…?" said Stjarna

"As far as they're concerned," said Eostre, pointing down towards the blue sky, "we're merely going to shoot plasma at the Earth, heating it up and turning the power back on."

The two soon expanded from third-dimensional nature to fourth-dimensional time as birds appeared flattened and frozen in place while high winds slowed to a halt. Eostre's ornate golden spacecraft, previously invisible, could now be plainly seen in its intricately carved splendor.

"Well, that's more within our grasp," said Stjarna, walking upwards toward the ship. "We'll really make a killing!"

They entered the ship door, where there were two lounge chairs and a control panel.

"You bet we will," said Eostre. "Now, let's go heat a planet!" She punched in a few buttons, and it darted through layers of the atmosphere.

The goddesses sat pretty in lounge chairs while the ship glided into outer space, and an ethereal blue field came closer and closer.

Eostre stopped the ship and turned it down to face a snowcapped blue and green marble.

"I hope you've rested well, because we've got a planet to warm," said Eostre, stepping out of the ship with Stjarna following close behind. They went back into nature; the gilded spaceship disappeared, and things bulged back out into three dimensions. Just as they planned, they unleashed a magnificent beam of white-hot plasma that wrapped around the Earth's atmosphere like a radioactive blanket.

All the lights above the membrane turned back on, for the divine city of Achtmorgen was just overhead. Clouds were now radiating heat with blindingly bright white glows seeping off of them. The goddesses' auras waned since they used up a lot of their power. They were panting and sweating plasma in exhaustion

"This better be worth it," said Stjarna. "I'm, like, beat."

"Don't worry about it," consoled Eostre. "It'll be super rewarding, trust me."

Months later, when summertime fully happened on Earth, Eostre and Stjarna were seen floating above the floor playing video games together in Eostre's gold and diamond mansion. The screen was made of crystal, and power flowed through white lines in the clean marble floors. A troupe of Elven butlers stood behind the two goddesses.

"Can't believe I ever doubted you," said Stjarna. "This is great."

"I'm a master at planning," bragged Eostre. "My mom is, like, the Queen of Fusion, so it kinda runs in the family."

"Matowits even convinced mortals that whatever those bird-winged people are called are sacred," chuckled Stjarna. "The non-winged mortals are even making totems in their honor!"

"That's adorable," said Eostre "Best we could manage was to tell those Elves that we talked to that they're from another planet."

"Speaking of which..." said Stjarna turning towards the butlers.

"Yes, mistress?" said the butler. "Thank you for giving me a place in Valhalla."

"You're welcome," said Eostre. "Now, make us a couple cups of juniper tea."

"Yes, mistress," stated the butler before walking through the hallway into one of the manor's smaller kitchens. On her walls were many portraits of Sun gods: Eostre's mother, Sol, who was a human goddess with pale white skin; Huizilopochtli, a human god with shining blue skin; and Ra, a tan-skinned human god with the brown and black feathered head of a falcon, his hooked black beak serving as the portrait's focal point.

The largest picture of all showed Eostre and Stjarna at a divine ball with other sharply dressed deities in an elaborately jeweled and decorated ballroom in the Sun. The mansion wasn't without similar splendor as it boasted bedrooms, bathrooms, elevators, and sculptures of ancient Solar aristocrats. Even the polished marbled floors crisscrossed blue, glowing lines of radioactive energy that had been etched into them so that every electrical device in the manor could work.

The butlers began to boil water using a kettle and a fire spell in the smallest kitchen of the mansion as Human maids dutifully dusted the elevator buttons and divine portraits. The head of the servants was an Angel with brown skin, dark red & gray wings and long black hair, as he wore the robe of a divine Lord. He could be seen looking through the magic mirrors, making sure the crew of servants were doing their jobs, when he saw a very peculiar god stepping out on to the lawn on all fours.

He got up and walked over towards an underground tunnel. Jumping in the air and opening his large wings, he took flight. He flapped his way forwards before banking straight up into a vacant elevator shaft that had an archway to Eostre's main living room. He hovered for a few moments until he perched his bare feet on the marble floor.

"Your Holiness," he said as Stjarna paused the game to look at him. "A creature is here to receive your blessing."

"I see," said Eostre, touching her feet to the floor. "Thank you, Te-meok."

"Not a problem, Your Holiness," replied Te-meok before he flew back down the shaft while Eostre and Stjarna opened the golden door. On the doorstep sat a howler monkey, small and brown-haired with a checkbook in hand.

"Hello, Your Majesty," he said.

"Hun Ahun," said Stjarna. "What brings you here?"

"I'm here to pay the electricity bill," replied the god. "Thanks, by the way, for restoring power to the lower EM belt."

"Anything to help the peasants," said Eostre. "Star-making is nothing to a Starlet like me."

Hun soon summoned a pen and wrote down his name in pictograms and an amount reading "12,000 Muons." Eostre swiftly grabbed the check and put it in her dress pocket.

"Thank you very much," she said as a one eyed raven landed on her lawn. "Your contribution will keep our miniature sun shining on."

"Glad I can help," said Hun with a childlike grin before he teleported away. Eostre was just about to close her door when Stjarna stopped her.

"Wait!" said Stjarna looking at the raven "I don't think it's a good idea to shut the door on him."

"You worry too much, Stjarna," bickered Eostre as the raven cawed at them, shrill and loud. One moment, there was a raven and the next, he'd lose his feathers, grow fingers, shortened his toes and split his beak apart into teeth that rapidly returned to his ever lightening mouth. Lips and a chin came back along with external genitalia while white hair and a matching long white beard instantly adorned his wrinkled chin. As a Human, he was strong and creepy looking with one left eye and an empty socket on his right.

"Eostre," said the god angrily. "I've come to give you a summons to court since you've sewn cataclysmic rapport!"

"But Allfather Odin," said Eostre, "why would we deal with mortals? They're retarded."

"The mortals needn't be portals for your selfish gain!" bickered Odin. "Your mother frowns upon your deed while ex-mortals drown in the briny waters of Earth to feed the seed of your twisted mirth!"

"We literally know nothing!" said Stjarna. "You're wasting your time."

"Insolent fools, I lust for all the knowledge of the universe," said Odin. "The Solar Mother entrusted me with a summons to court due to that apocalyptic issue that you need to sort!" Odin made a portal to a drab, slate interrogation room inside the Sun. It amounted to a stone box with only a narrow slit to let in the white-hot light of the radiative zone.

"You can't do this to us!" whined Stjarna

"'Tis punishment for crimes that need be decided, for you made the end times!" exclaimed Odin, making a forcefield in the manor's doorway. The magic forcefield repelled the two right into the portal like a sideways trampoline, and the two would end up in the room once the portal closed behind them.

Eostre tried firing plasma flames at the stone, but nothing happed, as her flares were as warm as the air around it.

"This isn't fair!" whined Eostre, banging on the stone wall. "This is my fucking birthstar. I can't be treated like a common criminal!"

"I told you from the start that this was a bad idea!" said Stjarna. "We'll be arrested and put in Hel's prison!"

"Mom wouldn't dare do that," she said. "She was always there to help me"

But just then, a shining, white goddess with blonde hair and chubby physique teleported into the interrogation room.

"Mom," said Eostre. "Thank goodness you're here. Odin's having us appear in trial… Maybe you can talk some sense into him."

"First of all, he rules our entire tribe of gods," said Sol, giving the two an angered, sneering look. "And second, that would result in a catastrophe far greater than what you two pulled off!"

Soon, two chairs shot ethereal chains at Eostre and Strjarna. The chains wrapped around their arms and torso before pulling them into the chairs—hard, diamond chairs. More chains would wrap around their legs once they were seated.

"We didn't do anything!" sobbed Stjarna.

"I've had the Berzerkers tell me otherwise!" exclaimed Sol with her hands on her hips. "Do you have any idea how much you ruined the last habitable planet?"

"You mean how we can provide a service to people left without electricity?" said Stjarna, feigning a mortified expression. "And make the planet more habitable for all those Elves and Ogres in the north!"

"That wasn't what Eostre told me when she started heating Earth's atmosphere," stated Sol with a smug smile on her face. "She called me up saying she was too lazy to power her own house."

"Mom, I expect to be liberated by my home, not restricted by it," said Eostre, rolling her eyes. "And besides, those stupid plasma spreads of yours burn asteroids to a crisp and leave the entire star system in the dark!"

"Eostre Glenrdottir!" exclaimed Sol, pointing at Eostre irately. "If I didn't launch all that plasma out of this star's corona, the Sun would've gone supernova. It would've obliterated all the planets in the Solar System, including their electromagnetic belts!"

Stjarna's face fell at the mere thought of her entire city and world being decimated in white fire. Eostre, meanwhile, had none of it.

"Mom, you've been doing this for what, four billion years? And you still resort to launching shit out into space!" she complained.

11

"And you are merely seventeen," retorted Sol. "You have no right to tell me how to do my job!"

"Well, I am great with hydrogen fusion!" gloated Eostre.

"Better than the ruler of the Sun?" asked Sol sourly.

"If something happens to you, I'll be the Queen of Fusion," said Eostre. "I don't deserve this treatment!"

"No one does," sighed Sol, "but I had to do what I had to do. It sucks that the power went out, but every god in the Solar System can make their own power in some capacity!"

Eostre groaned at this statement and rolled her eyes.

"You know what, Mom? I'm going to go to a new star and rule there with Stjarna," she said. "She's the only Star Deity around here who makes any sense!"

"Yeah!" proclaimed Stjarna, bolstering Eostre's point. "It's not like a little water hurt anyone."

"Your heating antics are melting the glaciers, unleashing millions of liters of seawater and flooding entire valleys, tribe lands & animals!" scolded Sol. "Not to mention all those deaths Odin has to deal with from…" she began counting up the causes of death on her fingers as she continued, "heatstroke, skin cancer, drowning, starvation, sodium poisoning & radiation poisoning!"

"But I didn't mean to cause so much suffering," said Eostre. "I just wanted to help people"

Sol immediately teleported them to separate jail cells with the ceiling of bars serving as a light source. The cells were miles away from each other in a Solar dungeon, a jail so large that it could only fit in the Sun's outer core. Stjarna looked up at the hallways of cells, making a vanishing point of squares in a long, angled, spiraling pattern of inmates on the walls, floor, and ceiling. They'd remain there for the next seven days until a muscular red-colored guards with eight muscular arms and brilliant red auras emanating from their body came to their cells.

The guard by Eostre slid the door with three hands before he proceeded to summon ethereal handcuffs on Eostre's wrists.

"Hey!" she exclaimed. "Where are you taking me!"

"I'm taking you to court," said the guard gruffly. "You've got some serious accusations laid against you, Eostre."

"Don't call me by name, peasant," said Eostre while being led into a portal that emptied into a large courtroom with monstrous spectators from many different pantheons. Stjrarna was in the aisle of spectators where Eostre had come in. She was just about to tell Stjarna how much she missed her until she saw who was behind the judge's podium.

There stood a very odd-looking man named Thoth who had the head of an ibis, teal feathers on his head and neck, two black beady eyes seemingly staring in two different directions, and a tan, Human body. His long, dark, curved beak counteracted it all as it made him appear dignified & stately. To the left and right of him were two witness stands and a jury box on Thoth's far left consisting of the most powerful aristocrats from all over the star system, including Odin and Sol.

"The case of Eostre Glenrdottir vs. the Sun System is now in session," announced Thoth, banging a bronze hammer on the podium. Everyone sat down as a couple of servants and bear monsters lined up behind the witness stands, waiting for the court slaves to give them truth serum to drink.

While the witnesses recanted what had happened, Eostre thought long and hard.

Maybe I could tell them about how I got the power back and that I would've been banished if I told everyone the truth, she thought. *Nah, Mom's in the jury, and she'd call me out behind my back. Maybe I'll go with a greater good argument. Thoth likes that stuff, and I could expand my following on Earth. Yeah, that's a great plan.*

Her face remained flat, as Eostre didn't want anyone to see her emotions, and she sat through a good hour of proceedings and statements from the guards who served as the prosecution before the sheep-headed slave gave Eostre a cup of truth serum, and she drank it.

"Your Majesty, Princess Eostre Glenrottr," said Thoth, looking down at her. "How do your plead?"

"I may well be guilty of mass murder, fraud, and solicitation," conceded Eostre, "but if I hadn't done it, then mortal life wouldn't have known about us. I mean, for millions of years, you've been allocated to different worlds until they became uninhabitable. Now that I've warmed the world with radiation, your dreams became a reality. And though it wasn't perfect, it at least bridged the gap between wildlife and the cosmos, so whatever you wanted to do with me, know that I, like, had a sound reason for doing the things I've done."

"And now we shall all begin our deliberation," said Thoth as he came down from the podium and joined the jurors. They walked out of the pew and into a back room overlooking the Sun's convective zone.

"What judgement best befits the goddesses two?" wondered Odin aloud. "For they stick together like glue."

"Well," stated Huitzilopochtli. "What are the divine casualties?" Ra looked at him with his beak agape in shock.

"Divine!" he boomed. "We're immortal, so I'm more concerned about how those two ruined Earth!"

"There be a million deaths, some from the land dweller's last breath," said Odin, "betwixt burning and starving."

"As terrible as it is," said Apollo, a pinkish, pale Human god with brown hair and green eyes, "we've been able to give these smart animals new life and careers with the help of Hades and Hel."

"As much as it pains me to say this," sighed Sol, "he's right; they'd be a bunch of amnesiacs without us."

"So we're just going to ignore the fact that your daughter is a fucking con artist!" exclaimed Bochica, who had tan skin and long, black hair.

"We're not ignoring a thing," said Odin. "'Tis quite brash to do that sort of accusing!"

"You fruity Aesirs with your poetry mead!" exclaimed Ra, motioning to Odin. "Why would you guys take orders from a man who can't stop rhyming?"

"He can't help it!" exclaimed Sol, remembering why Ra commands a different portion of the Sun. "Since he drank it all, his entire body has become pure poetry. He was young and geeky then!"

"Oh, so you're defending the thieving actions of your Emperor now," quipped Bochica, pouting sourly, "just like you to steal and conquer us Enneads?"

"Maybe if you guys hadn't been so stupid and barbaric, Mars would still be green now!" bickered Apollo.

15

"Don't forget who is King around here!" said Ra angrily, summoning a solar disc to the top of his head. "If you wanna throw down in the vacuum of space, I'll gladly burn your ass into submission, Earth-brain!"

"Enough!" exclaimed Thoth, casting binding magic on all their mouths and throats, forcing them to be silent. "I'm among the self-birthed first generation in the universe. I don't need such petty bickering when our sentence will affect the structure of the Aesir government! Now, I'm going to let you all speak, but only about what which pertains to the legality of their sentencing, got it!"

They all nodded uncomfortably, realizing that they were kids millions and billions of years old before the wise eyes of a primordial cosmic grandfather.

"Good" said Thoth, stroking the sides of his long beak. "Now, tell me what's best for Princess Eostre and her accomplice."

The was a long silence as uncomfortable gazes shot all over the room with angry gods staring down each other.

"Maybe transformation would be best," suggested Bochica before the other gods gazed at him speechlessly. "It worked with Huitaca, and as an owl, she's the happiest she's been in her entire life. If they want to be with Earthlings, they should live like Earthlings!"

"But Huitaca was just a nuisance to us," said Apollo "These two are making the last habitable planet in the star system drown in salt water!"

"The sheltered people be blind," said Odin, "with water-borne continents leaving the knowledge of the smart folks in a bind!"

"I've always like worlds with interconnected continents," lamented Thoth, tilting his long neck down in silence. "It encourages a larger variety of people and animals that way"

"If they shelter the world," said Ra getting an idea, "then we could shelter them from us."

Thoth tapped the sharp end of his beak.

"Hmm…" he said. "Maybe by banishing them to an isolated asteroid."

"I rather they be in the Sun," said Odin, "for the Sun was their birthstar where they should never stray very far."

"They're half star," said Thoth. "It's better, in my time-honored wisdom, that they're hot creatures, so being where it's cold would be the greatest of tortures for them to feel what all of those peasant gods and mortals felt."

Odin paused and considered it.

"'Tis an idea extraordinaire to leave them where there's no air."

"It seems we've reached a consensus," said Thoth, tilting his head up and out as the jury of royals nodded their heads. They all came out of the room, Thoth resuming to the podium and the jurors returning to the benches.

"After much deliberation," announced Thoth formally, "I hereby sentence Eostre and Stjarna to banishment." He banged his hammer against the podium, opening up two wormholes right in the middle of the courtroom.

"This is bull!" exclaimed Sol. "This is their birthstar. You can't just banish them like this!"

"We've already agreed!" exclaimed Thoth wrathfully. "Your daughter is almost a grown woman. She can look after herself!"

Thoth made two portals as a large row broke out among the divine spectators.

"Join my army if you want to make the birdbrain judges pay!" exclaimed Sol to the attendees of the trial. The two Princesses were drawn to the portals as though they were black holes. They vanished into them before the portals phased out of existance in a matter of milliseconds.

"No!" exclaimed Sol "She's not ready to be beyond the inner four. She needs to be trained on the affairs of the outer Solar System!"

"Under guidance of our royal scribe!" exclaimed Bochica "Your precious little Princess will get a healthy dose of responsibility!"

"Easy for you to say!" said Apollo "If we detained Prince Geb to a deserted moon somewhere, you'd be just as distraught!"

"He left the nest like 30,000 years ago," defended Ra. "Besides he wouldn't be nearly as irresponsible as Eostre!"

"The guy used to think devistating earthquakes were funny." said Eostre "But because he's your Prince, you want to make excuses for him!"

"We've reached a verdict, you two!" complained Thoth coming between them and splitting them up. "Justice is justice and the Aesir tribe is far too blinded by wrath to see that this needed to happen."

"The Ennead tribe left our sanity sore," rebutted Odin. "The only choice we've got is 't declare war on you lot!"

"Then let's raise armies and fight in the inner asteroid belt" said Thoth "For Solar land claims for the Aesir Sun Princess." He concentrated the beam at Odin causing the two to vanish into thin air and the other gods followed a split second later. Sol raised an army of berzerkers, wolves and horses while Ra would raise an army of minor warrior deities, scarabs and chimeric monsters.

As far as Eostre knew, she was instantly put on a greyish-tan asteroid far away from sunlight or any other asteroids.

"No! Stjarna! Mom!" she exclaimed with despair. "You were supposed to let me off!" She shot a plasma beam to the core of the asteroid, only to have it heal up in a matter of seconds "You've got to be fucking with me!" she exclaimed. "I don't belong on some lowly rock!" She stepped over an ice hill and landed on the other side due to the asteroid's low gravity.

"No one," she said tearing up. "Stjarna!" she called, only to hear the deafening sound of silence. She was put in the realm of nature well beyond the reach of any mortals. The Springtime Goddess sniffled and laid down in the dirt sobbing and bawling tears of plasma that would only become icy stardust comets in the intense cold of deep space.

Everything was lost, her servants, her mansion and her control.

I might as well be dead… she thought to herself, shivering as the ice hills melted into a sphere of water. "Why me!" she said. "I'm a royal—not a lowly plant!" she said, then she cried herself to sleep.

"Hello?" said a gruff sounding voice as Eostre opened her eyes to a rather unusual-looking god. He was as black as nightfall with a curved muzzle filled with razor-sharp teeth, two wide red eyes, and long rectangular ears. He stood over Eostre nude and barefoot. "I can't help but notice your struggles," he said, trying to sound kind.

"I miss Stjarna," said Eostre, sobbing. "I miss being in line for the throne, and I miss my mansion!"

"I know how you feel," said the god as he took a couple steps closer to Eostre. "I ruled the Sun System millions of years ago."

Her eyes lit up at that.

"Really?" she asked. "What happened?"

"Well, all the others said I was a freak, and they banished me," he said. "Part antelope, part jackal, part aardvark, part anteater, and part rabbit… The name's Set, by the way."

"Hello Set," said Eostre sadly. "Thanks for talking to me."

"It's from one aristocrat to another," said Set, showing a mouthful of razor-sharp teeth in a sinister grin. "Don't be afraid of me."

"I'm not," replied Eostre. "I've had Angels, monkeys, and dragons kneeling at my feet. You're nothing compared to what goes on in the Sun."

"Glad to hear it," said Set getting out a bottle of gin and taking a sip. "Anyways, they shunned me away to this asteroid field, just like you, and you know what I did?"

"What?" asked Eostre, sitting at the edge of a rock

"The King of the Kmetics was Osiris in those days," explained Set "He and Thoth banished me for thousands of years in the red deserts of Mars, so I assassinated the bastard—chopped him up into bits and fed his dick to some fish."

Eostre looked at Set with terror with her jaw dropped.

"Your lucky I'm part star," she said in an act of intimidation. "I'd blow you up along with this asteroid if you tried to come near me!"

"Oh, but I wouldn't dream of harming a beautiful little goddess like yourself," said Set. "I've changed since then. I've served my time, and I offer guidance to other banished deities."

"And what do you think I should do?" asked Eostre "I can't talk with mortals and I'm probably not allowed in a 6,000 kilometer radius of the Sun."

"Just show 'em who's boss," said Set. "The thing with Osiris sounds grim, but when you consider that he led a genocide and a pogrom of ethnic cleansing against my people, it was the only way I could get them to listen. I even sicced a giant snake to keep him from being resurrected while I put the Sun System through a Golden Age until I handed the throne to Ra once things normalized."

"Yeah, but I don't know if I could…" she said. "I mean, I only wanted the power to come back on. It's as not as bad as what you went through, though."

"Well, why don't you drink my enchanted brew?" said Set, passing her the bottle of gin. "It's a warrior's potion I made to bolster my courage and strength. You're a Princess; you're practically predestined to rule the Sun. I was a mere peasant god standing up to a tyrant."

"You know what?" she said, snatching the gin out of Set's hand. "I was meant to rule. I'll show them." She soon began to chug the whole bottle of gin in one go, but what she didn't know was that Set was a trickster god and compulsive liar.

The Asteroid Belt was a prominent battlefield where the warring factions shot magic blasts and cosmic artillery on the astral plane. The soldiers nobly fought, with many being killed on the battlefield and a chorus of gunfire persisting at random points on the battlefield. The bear-like Berzerkers roared a primal battle cry as the six-armed Scarabs fired guns and launched grenades simultaneously.

There was armageddon in the asteroid belt as the ethereal plane became the ethereal pits. Berzerkers bit warrior gods, and flying Dire Wolves threw hellfire bombs down onto the battlefield, launching smoke and flame to all who stood near.

"You fuckwits never listened to your Princess!" exclaimed Eostre in a frenzy. "This is what y'all get for not listening to the Aesirs!" Soon, she wrangled smaller asteroids with a beam of plasma and hurled them at random parts of the battlefield.

The flying asteroids crashed into soldiers of either faction faster than the speed of sound, killing them on impact. Not even an Angel's bombs could blast away the asteroids in time. Eostre laughed maniacally as her asteroids wiped out entire regiments. Horses futilely tried to dodge the asteroids, even as they crashed into each other, making even smaller shards of rock and metal. Cosmic shrapnel overpowered the battlefield with the ever-present sight of clouding death and dismemberment everywhere they turned until they were next.

But by the time General Glenr caught wind of Eostre's antics, she had gone into an uncharted area of spirit heaven that was grey and uninhabited, save for the freshly made ghosts. Eostre blasted a plasma spread on the ghosts, decimating them into nonexistence so that no witnesses would spoil her plan. She soon made a portal to what would now be Lower Saxony in northwestern Germany, where a wild rabbit could be seen birthing her litter.

She cast a spell on the rabbit, endowing divine powers into the last of the litter of seven.

"That'll show 'em who's boss," she chortled as she proceeded to irradiate the bunny, the last of which would be snow-white as opposed to greyish-brown. "You'll serve me well someday," she said, picking up the white kit and petting it.

The End

2

THE LANDING

Seventy-eight years before the settlement of Plymouth Rock sailed three great wooden galleons up the Pacific Ocean on an expedition of the new world. The ships were named San Miguel, La Victoria, and the largest of them all was called San Salvador. They transported knights in shining armor, their horses, tents, weapons, and their Captain, Juan Cabrillo.

He was busy working in the captain's deck on the first map of California as a Duke with a long, straight mustache, a pointed goatee, and colorful garments sat next to him as Juan dipped a long feather pen in a brass vial of black ink.

"California is at an odd longitude away from the rest of America," he stated

"Well, Juan, this must be another island like Cuba," he said. "But not all of these lands would make good colonies."

"I know, Your Grace," said Juan as he sketched a line on the other side of the California coast. "But that's what they said before I found gold in Guatemala!"

"The tribesmen better not be leading us astray!" he said as Juan continued the line from the tip of Baja California up past a bay labeled San Miguel. "If I'm going to rule this island as Viceroy, there has to be something I can send to the rest of the empire!"

"Don't worry, Your Grace," said Juan, making a rough slash-mark shape on the paper. "If you survive the expedition, you can always go back to being a Duke in the old world."

"Please, Salamanca is a living hell right now!" he said, rubbing his temples as Juan put the pen back in its vial. "Well…new continent, new opportunities," shrugged the Duke as Juan got up.

"I'm going to go check on my crew, Your Grace," said Juan as he proceeded to walk out of the Captain's quarters down to the main deck. The crew members were busy cleaning moss from the from the ship's wooden floorboards and measuring the ship's speed with knots of rope.

"Have you found any other islands yet?" asked Juan.

"Yes, sir," replied the crew member, looking down at his compass. "There's an island to the northwest over there, and another one due north up here." He pointed to two faint mounds in the distance.

"Let's dock on the northward isle. It looks larger."

"Yes, sir," said the crew member as Juan walked up toward the galleon's steering wheel.

"Land ho!" he announced. "Eight degrees on the port bow." Most of the crew members looked toward the larger island before they proceeded to climb down one of the ship's ladders into the lower deck. A few of them remained on the upper deck as Juan asked, "Ensign, what's the ship's speed?"

"We're at about 15 knots, sir," replied the Ensign.

"Thank you," said Juan, then he turned to another crew member. "Hey Coxcox, lower the mainsail."

"Yes, sir," replied Coxcox as he clambered up a ladder of rope up toward the mainsail, unhooking it from the mast. Juan, meanwhile, steered the ship closer and closer to the island until a small beach with brownish green hills came into view. Crew members walked back onto the main deck and proceeded to lower the anchor once they got close enough. The other ships in the fleet would stop nearly a few hundred meters away from the San Salvador.

Juan disembarked along with the crew on modest rowboats until they reached the beach. Slowly but surely, all the sailors from the San Salvador got their horses and the Centaur knights off the galleons and onto the island.

"Let's set up camp before we go any further," said Juan. "God knows what's lurking up here."

"Yes, sir," said the crewmen as they pitched tents while crews of other ships brought food, water, and other supplies before they went back to join their respective Captains. The Duke came to the outpost on his own dinghy with a Catholic Priest and the man rowing it.

"Isn't it beautiful?" said Juan

"It's a blessing that we're here," stated the Priest as he and the Duke got off the boat

"Indeed," said the Duke "But don't get your hopes up, Juan, this is only a mere expedition."

"I know, Your Grace," he said to the Duke "But this is the Eden of the New World. Think about it: arable soil for crops, a long, flat beach for a dock, seas on all sides to create a fort, no sign of natives, and good weather."

"Yes, it's so refreshing to be in cool climate after having been in the jungle so long," said the Priest "And who knows? Perhaps the city of Eldorado is up here."

"But there's still no city of Eldorado!" exclaimed the Duke "I mean, what would we even call the fort anyways!"

"San Salvador sounds good," replied Juan. "Yeah, this island is a gift from Christ, the savior, so San Salvador would be a fantastic name for this island. It'll serve as the capital of Upper California with you, Your Grace, as its Viceroy!"

"San Salvador is the name of your ship!" interjected the Duke "We haven't even found Eldorado, so what makes you think that this will be the Eden of the New World?"

"Patience, Your Grace," bickered Juan. "It's bound to be somewhere!"

"Very well, but I still have my doubts," remarked the Duke as they all went their separate ways and the crew members finished setting up camp.

"Your Grace," said Juan a few minutes later, "how might you like to go surveying the land with us?"

"I'd like to see what's actually here, so sure," replied the Duke before Juan turned towards his crew.

"I need ten horsemen to scout the land with us!" he said, remembering the casualties of the previous encounters with other tribes. "We don't want to start a war until we claim the land, alright?"

"Yes, sir!" said the crewmen. Ironclad Centaurs simply got up while the remaining seven Human cavalry had to mount their horses, some doing it quicker than others.

"Father," said Juan, turning toward the Priest, "I want you to divine information for the men here at base camp, so they can know about savage tribes that could ambush us."

"Of course, I will," stated the Priest "You can always count on me."

Juan soon turned towards his mounted crew and commanded: "Men, you are to follow me and serve as a backup in case me or His Grace don't survive the expedition."

"Yes, sir!" they said, following Juan uphill through the tall, yellow grass and groves of cypress trees.

Juan made a mental note of the terrain as the Duke quietly admired his surroundings, but just as he was about to say something, he came across a small village with reed tents and about 15 people present. They all stared in awe at the settler's clothes, armor and their brown-coated beasts. The natives spoke to each other in Tongva. They spoke in tones of fear and anxiety before it turned to anger. One of them bickered to the Elder as they all pointed at the horses.

"Don't worry," said the Duke in calming tones. "We only mean harm when you want to war." He swiped his hands down to show that they came in peace.

The Elder calmed the villagers down as he got a dark yellow potion in a wooden bowl out of his hut, which was the largest in the village. He pointed at the Duke as he continued speaking to the villagers in more confident tones. Both Juan and the Duke looked on speechless at what lay before them, ready to retreat at the first sign of attack. The elder walked toward the Duke and presented the bowl.

"Nawishko Miha," he said.

"Well, certainly better than what we had back in San Miguel," remarked Juan

"Should I take it?" asked the Duke turning towards Juan.

"I would," replied Juan. "It's probably some kind of peace offering."

"Well, I don't want to start anything yet," said the Duke before he took the potion and drank all of it. It tasted sweet like juice as the Duke grinned at the villagers. "Thank you," said the Duke, giving the bowl back to the Elder. The Elder took it and nodded before the party walked away.

They trekked on a system of trails and footpaths made by the natives as they continued to walk through villages where locals seemingly ignored them as they passed through. The villages had bonfires that were alive and flickering as they were busy sending smoke signals to the other neighboring villages. The artisans each took a piece a sea lion pelt and covered the flames before removing it, so they could create patterns in the smoke.

The Duke, meanwhile, began to change as his overcoat drooped down over his narrowing shoulders while his neck gradually extended to become became longer and longer. The next village was at the opposite tip of the island. By the time the explorers came, there were warriors with flaming spears and arrows in their arsenal at the ready for the party.

"Retreat, they're armed!" exclaimed Juan as they ran behind the horsemen, who all galloped into the distance.

The Duke shrank, and his clothes became baggier. He kept pulling up his pantaloons as he ran. His fingers gradually began to lose sensation as they stiffened. Once Juan caught his breath, he noticed that the Duke was long necked and hunched over as he struggled to keep his pantaloons on his ever-fattening waist. Juan stared at the Duke as his moustache and hair fell off his ever-shrinking head.

"Y-Your Grace?" said Juan. "You look kind of strange"

"What, oh no-no-no-no, I'm norm al," stammered the Duke as Juan noticed that his arms were stiffening and his fingers were fusing together.

"Let's get you to the Priest. Those villagers probably put a curse on you!" exclaimed Juan

"N-n-no that's fal-al-al-alse," he gobbled as he followed Juan back to the camp. His neck wrinkled and his lips pursed backwards. He bent downwards as his ruffled collar fell onto the ground, that the Duke proceeded to trample over. By the time he got to the camp, everyone gazed in fear as the Duke's fatty form was revealed and small spines emanated from his body.

"Y-Your Grace, you're becoming a monster!"

"Y-y-you are-ar-ar-ar the monsh tersh!" he gobbled as his teeth exceeded his lips revealing his teeth melting and fusing to become a brownish hooked beak. He fell out of his shoes, revealing an extra toe seemingly growing out from the balls of his feet. The spines gained brownish red fibers as he ran over to Juan and pecked at him while the Duke's eyes became darker and moved to the sides of his ever-balding head.

Horrified, the Priest uttered an incantation in Latin "O Holy Father, lift the curse off his grace, Duke Jorge and keep him in a Human shape" yellow divine light appeared from the cross on his staff until it whisped away with the wind vanishing into air.

He watched in horror as the Duke's legs gained scales and feathers dominated his ever shrinking body. "What's going on, Your Holiness!" exclaimed Juan "Does the Father not wish to help him!"

The former Duke gave into his instincts and started pecking at the crew members while displaying his ever feathering tail to scare off the evil monsters. The Priest would see a vision of God who looked like a long white haired Angel with a long white beard and wearing a Papal robe. He would appear hovering above a grassy hillside "Let this be, my Child." said God. "I've destined him to a much greater position than any worldly royal family."

God would vanish as the Duke's transformation was complete. He was now a normal, if hostile, turkey attacking intruders of their territory. Juan, the Priest and a couple crew members shooed the turkey off into some nearby bushes. "If these people can make His Grace into an exotic bird" said Juan shaken by the experience "Who knows what they'll do to us"

"The Lord Appeared in a Revalation just now" said the Priest looking down at an empty mound of royal clothing that lie in the sand "His Grace was destined to live as a beast not as a man and it's a sign from the Heavens that we're not supposed to settle here."

With those words ringing in their heads, they all left the island of San Salvador the very next day. The Duke was no longer Jorge of Salamanca in the crown of Castille; now, they were a hermaphroditic turkey that could lay their own eggs without ever breeding with another turkey.

Later that same voyage, Juan would go on to discover what we'd now call Santa Barbara, San Luis Obispo, the San Francisco Bay, the Monterey Bay, Mendocino, and Eureka.

Cabrillo went back to San Salvador to more accurately survey the island. Him and his crew were met with hostility from the tribesmen. The ex-duke had gained a new name from the encounter, Pimu. By the time Juan came back, they had relearned to talk with a beak. They swore at Juan, and the natives shot a flaming arrow at Juan's thigh. The crewmen got back to the ship and sailed off. The encounter had left him with an open gash that became gangrenous, and he subsequently died at age 43.

The places Cabrillo discovered would not gain permanent settlements for over a century after his death. He was embalmed, and his remains were buried in San Salvador, or Catalina Island as we'd call it today. San Miguel is now known as San Diego, as Juan's legacy was largely lost and remains overshadowed by other explorers and conquerors who took the same risks as he did.

Pimu, on the other hand, learned spiritual magic and gave their eggs to other warring tribes that always hatched into perfectly healthy chicks. Pimu is now among the most powerful Wizards in California. You might've even seen them walking around in the San Gabriel mountains. Pimu's children are all enchanted with a special magic that activates as soon as they're eaten on the day of Thanksgiving.

The moment you split the wishbone and you're truly grateful in your mind and body, Pimu will grant your wish and make your wildest dreams come true. Those who find themselves ungrateful will have back luck and misfortune befall them.

The End

3

THE BALLAD OF KONSTANTINOS II

Once upon a time, there was a King named Konstantinos who lived in a great palace in the middle of Athens. Two flags proudly blew in the wind on top of the palace gates. The flags had a dark blue background, a thick white cross splitting it up into four even quadrants as a pictogram of a golden crown sat dead center. All buildings in the palace complex were large, spacious, and painted white with an elaborate neoclassical style of architecture as a show of ancient Greek heritage.

The royal family that called this palace home sat down at breakfast and the King, Konstantinos was reading the newspaper as usual. The King was a tall, intimidating Tauren with black fur, stocky build, and imposing white horns that framed his golden jeweled crown.

He was only 26 but had already reigned for three years along with his 20-year-old wife, Queen Anne-Marie whose white fur had many large black spots as her relatively thin physique was disrupted by her stomach that bulged outward with a baby, her horns were mere yellowish spikes hidden under her own, smaller golden jeweled crown.

She readied a bowl of oatmeal before their 20-month old daughter, a far less spotted, pink nosed Princess, Alexia. Anne-Marie also set a sippy cup full of her own milk on Alexia's high chair before she sat down before her own breakfast. The headline "Beatles perform live in Athens" and a grainy monochrome picture of the rock group performing stared back at her.

"Well, how do you like that!" exclaimed Konstantinos as Anne-Marie turned her snout towards the King's direction.

"What is it, sweetie?" asked Anne-Marie

"They're saying that I'm selfish and out of touch because of what I did to Parliament!" exclaimed Konstantinos. "I know that people in my kingdom are suffering, but they should be grateful to live in the last free market in Eastern Europe!"

"Why do you even read those civilian newspapers anyways!" complained the Queen "We have informants, y'know."

"I just need to know how my subjects become informed on what happens here," said the King pointing straight down to the table. "Because I am not out of touch—heck, we invite the Kristakises to watch TV here in the palace since they're not lucky enough to own one!"

"Is Daddy tubble?" asked Alexia

"I'll tell you when you're older. Now, drink your milk," said Anne-Marie.

"If you're still the Princess that is…" muttered Konstantinos under his breath before taking another bite of his waffles and maple syrup.

"I'm sorry, sweetie, what was that?" asked the Queen turning her ear in the King's direction.

"Oh," said Konstantinos. "It's nothing."

"Ah," said Anne-Marie as Alexia put her sippy cup down on the tray of her high chair. The Queen soon sat in her own chair, rubbing her bulging stomach. The King, meanwhile, remained silent as he continued eating before setting his newspaper to one side of the table. He looked down in silence, keeping his face stoic as not to alarm his family, even if it meant having a looming silence over each of their shoulders.

"Done," stated Alexia as Konstantinos stood up from his chair with one corner of waffle left. He got a handkerchief out of his suit pocket and proceeded to wipe his muzzle of maple syrup before folding it back up and placing it back into his pocket. He walked over towards Alexia's high chair saying with a smile.

"That's good, but I have to go work now."

"Already?" inquired Anne-Marie, looking at an ornate grandfather clock that stood in the royal dining hall. "It's barely quarter till nine."

"I'm a very busy man," said Konstantinos. "Somebody has to keep this country together."

"Okay, Your Highness," chuckled Anne-Marie.

Konstantinos turned toward Alexia and told her, "Now, no matter what happens, just remember that you'll always be Daddy's little Princess," before nuzzling the side of her furred head and kissing her on the cheek.

Alexia smiled and chuckled at the gesture.

"And what do you say?" asked Anne-Marie as Alexia's smile turned flat. "Say thank you," prompted the Queen.

"Tank you," repeated the Princess as the King walked towards the door saying, "If anyone needs me, I'll be in the royal office."

"Say bye to Daddy," said Anne-Marie.

"Bye Daddy," repeated Alexia as Konstantinos shut the door behind him. He walked past the throne. His hoofbeats were dampened by a lavish Persian rug as he walked past landscapes, portraits of previous kings and white marble sculptures of gods and leaders made by ancient Athenians.

He walked down a flight of marble stairs to a great hall with large windows on the left-hand side of the hall and doors to the offices of Cabinet Ministers on the right-hand side. Brass nameplates glistened in the morning sun, interspersed with oil paintings and shining golden door handles. He stopped at the office labeled 'HH Konstantinos II.'

He turned toward the door before pressing the handle down and pulling it open, revealing a very spacious office with two black leather chairs in front of a large wooden desk with multiple typed reports and bills, a beige electric typewriter, a black rotary phone, and a wooden shelf sat in the back left corner of the room.

He sat down in an office chair before opening up the desk drawer and getting out his ballpoint pen, so he could sign bills into law while vetoing others. Some came from Greek Parliament while others came from the Prime Minister.

"Not bad for your first month," he muttered as he reached for the handle on the shelf, flipping it down, revealing a built-in two band radio and turntable. He soon turned it on and the record changer cracked into life as its tubes warmed up, the turntable rotated and the stylus automatically moved to the record's run in. Following a few seconds of surface noise, rock music soon started playing through the stereo's speakers.

He kept working through paperwork like this for the better part of two hours, occasionally changing inputs to the radio if he came across something especially objectionable. But just as he got to the last of the daily paperwork, the phone started ringing, and the King got up and lifted the stylus off the playing record and guided it back into its default position. He sat back down and picked up the phone.

"Konstantinos the Second, King of the Hellenes speaking."

"Hello, Your Highness," greeted a voice on the other end of the line. "This is Pavlo Demetrios, Minister of Internal Affairs, and your recent antics have warranted great concern from all of us in the Cabinet."

"So I appointed some parliamentarians. It's a hell of a lot better than having a bunch of socialists running around my Parliament proposing orwellian tyranny!" said Konstantinos.

"Your Highness!" replied the Minister. "That violates the Greek Constitution of 1952, which clearly states that the ruling monarch can't interfere with public election. Not to mention your firing of Prime Minister Tsirimokos!"

"You think I wanted to be the fucking King!" bickered Konstantinos. "My father had stomach cancer for Christ sakes, and now my goddamn country is in chaotic peril; and the chaos, I might add, comes from beyond the northern border!"

"I'm sorry about that, Your Highness," said the Minister, "but we have these things in place for a reason!"

"Yes, yes, of course. I took that oath at my coronation," said Konstantinos, rubbing his forehead.

"So you know that parliamentarians are supposed to represent the Greek people here in Athens and that people en masse vote for a candidate to influence an outcome," explained the Minister

"Yes, that is the idea behind a constitution," said Konstantinos. "But—"

"You want to control the country from the top down," said Pavlo, "like those communist dictatorships you seem so hell bent on Greece not becoming."

Konstantinos sighed, saying, "Listen, the CIA is counting on me to ensure that my people are free and prosperous. The people I appoint have a clean record—unlike the power grubbing jackasses that the Thracians wish to be in power."

"Has it ever occurred to you, Your Highness, that maybe they vote like that because you fulfil the narrative of the bourgeois King oppressing the agricultural proletariat?" questioned Pavlo.

"Hmm," pondered Konstantinos stroking his muzzle. "I suppose you're right, and if it's alright with Prime Minister Kanellopoulos, I want to schedule an election."

"Great, so when were you thinking?" asked the Minister.

"I was perhaps thinking the twenty-seventh of May," said the King "It should give them plenty of time to campaign."

"Great!" exclaimed the Minister. "I'll pass it along to Kanellopoulos."

"Right, I'll talk to you later," said the King

"Bye," replied the Minister before hanging up.

Konstantinos then hung up before he moved the stylus back on the start of the record and soon got back to work. He got to the last of the bills around 30 minutes later as the player was on the last in the stack of records when the phone rang once more, and just like the last time, he put the stylus back to the holder, and the record stopped spinning. He answered, "Konstantinos the Second, King of the Hellenes speaking."

"This is General Papadopoulos, and I wish to speak with you immediately," stated the voice on the phone.

"Very well," said the King with a look of apprehension. "You have the level of clearance, so why don't you meet me on the throne?"

"Alright," said the General "I'll meet you there, bye."

"Bye," replied the King as the General hung up. The King put the phone back onto the base unit before turning off the stereo and walking out of the office. He walked back through the hallway up the marble stairs before sitting down on his ornately crafted throne with wooden appointments and a plush back. He sat there looking at his sculpture collection until hoofbeats could be heard climbing up the stairs, and up came Gen. Georgios Papadopoulos a stern-looking man in a deep blue uniform with a white leather sash. He had a small white moustache, thinning black hair broken up by curved, goat-like horns, and a nose that was just as pointed as his long ears.

"General," said the King "What do you wish to discuss?"

"Your Highness, I would like to discuss ways to keep your royal family safe," stated the General.

"Now is the best time," said Konstantinos. "I mean, all the letters my secretaries have been getting, I don't know who to trust anymore!"

"Well, I command the army who defend you with their lives, Your Highness," said the General. "You can always rely on me."

"I suppose," said the King "Now, what were your ideas?"

"As you are aware, Your Highness, marxist guerrilla forces have been plaguing many countries around the world," said the General "even though we haven't had anything like that here since the Civil War; they've all gone underground."

"Go on," said the King, nodding his head

"They're still as virulent in their beliefs now as they were back then, and they've made it their goal to assassinate you!" said the General.

"Where did you get this from?" inquired the King

"I have received intel from our undercover operatives" stated the general. "Whichever one gets at you first will be the one to stage their second civil war."

"Oh!" said Konstantinos. "Is there any solution?"

"Now, how many cars do you have here in the complex?" asked Georgios.

"I would say five if you count the limousine," stated Konstantinos. "Why do you want to know?"

"Because when it comes high time to go on speaking tour, you can't park them too close to the street; at least not without having more security in the area," said the General.

"I suppose," said Konstantinos, mulling it over. "And is there anywhere else that might be vulnerable to assassins?"

"Now, Your Highness, the royal bedroom is facing the street, right?" asked Georgios.

"It's up on the 5th floor, but yes, I have a view of the civilian apartments," said Konstantinos.

"Well, Your Highness, it might be an eyesore in the morning, but it would be worth it to you to have the blinds open," stated Georgios.

"And why is that?" asked Konstantinos.

"So it doesn't look like a bedroom. As far as the assassins would be concerned, it's just another office," explained the General.

"I see," said Konstantinos. "Thank you very much for bringing it to my attention."

"Not a problem, Your Highness," said the General "I'll see you around."

"You too," replied the King as the General walked back out of the throne room and down the stairs.

In the palace garden, where there were flowers, fountains, and brick walkways, Anne-Marie was watching her daughter run around the play structure, soiling her dress in the process. The Princess soon stood still once she noticed her father walking out of the palace at a brisk walking pace. Once he was closer, she ran over to him, saying: "Daddy, pay wimme!"

"Sorry, Alexia, I have business to attend to with Mommy," he said, walking toward Anne-Marie. "Honey, we need to talk," said Konstantinos in a fearful tone.

"What happened?" asked the Queen

"In private," clarified the King

"But what about Alexia?" asked Anne-Marie.

"There's plenty of guards on patrol right now. They have to keep watch of all of the family," said the King as he looked to the nearby guard. "Excuse me, Michalis. Would you mind watching Her Majesty while we talk?"

"Of course, Your Highness," said the toga-clad guard as the King got up and motioned the Queen to follow him.

The two soon walked past a fountain back into the palace, where there was a small conversation room with several paintings and photographs of previous kings as well as a fully decked out component hi-fi with a turntable, a reel-to-reel tape deck, and a three-band radio.

"Listen, I was just speaking to the General in the throne room," said Konstantinos.

"What happened?" said Anne-Marie concerned,

"He asked me about how many cars I had and where we sleep," explained Konstantinos.

"So?" asked Anne-Marie.

"Don't you find it suspicious," suggested the King "that he might want to know these specific things?"

"I'm sure that there's a sensible reason for this," stated Anne-Marie.

"Well, he said he was worried about guerrillas," explained Konstantinos. "But this isn't anything like how it was for you in Denmark. We've had civil wars and opposing ideologies practically since the day of our first constitution."

"I realize that," said Anne-Marie. "But why don't you just call the NIS? They're certain to get this all straightened out."

"Y'know," said Konstantinos, "that's a great idea, I wish I thought of it!"

"Thanks," said Anne-Marie. "Anything to keep the dynasty together."

"I'll go to talk to them, and you can just take it easy for now," said Konstantinos, walking out of the conversation room and into the first level hallway where there was a golden chandelier and several landscapes as a black wall phone sat between two pictures. He took the handle off the base unit and turned the phone's rotor with his thick, black hand before holding it up to the side of his head while the other end gave an intermittent tone until someone answered.

"Elias Mikos, Chairman of the NIS speaking"

"This is Konstantinos the Second, King of the Hellenes, and I was wondering how many agents there were undercover," said the King.

"We have no agents undercover, Your Highness," stated the Chairman.

"Funny, General Papadopoulos told me that you lot had agents investigating underground terror cells," said the King

"There haven't been those kinds of terror cells in 15 years, Your Highness," stated the Chairman.

"Well then!" said the King. "Is he, say, planning any meetings?"

"Let me just check, Your Highness," stated the Chairman as the line became silent with a slight thud. After a good minute, the Chairman returned, saying, "We have letters to and from the General as well as the Minister of Defense that a meeting will take place this afternoon."

"I see, could you possibly send over Patriarch Eugenius?" said the King "I want to be able to perform some surveillance."

"Understandable, Your Highness," stated the Chairman. "I'll send him over at the earliest convenience."

"Right," said the King "Goodbye, then."

"Goodbye, Your Highness," said the Chairman as Konstantinos hung up.

Several hours later, the King sat down in the family chamber before a 55cm TV, tapping his fingers on his navy blue slacks.

Eventually, a door opened, and in came the Patriarch of the Greek Orthodox Church, who was 186 years old and had a long, black beard. He wore a humble-looking black and red robe as well as a large staff topped by a golden Orthodox cross being firmly held in his left hand.

"So good to see you, Your Holiness," said Konstantinos, kneeling in his presence.

"Likewise," said Eugenius. "Now, how might I be of service?"

"I have suspicions that General Papadopoulos is betraying me," said the King "I want you to make the TV show the meeting in Parliament, so I can see what they're planning."

"Of course, but would you mind tuning the TV to channel six, so I can divine a clearer image?" asked the Patriarch

"Of course, Your Holiness," said Konstantinos, getting up and turning the tuner from channel one to six with a great metallic click with each turn of the dial. He pulled the power button outward, and the tubes came to life with a subtle hum. First came loud white noise and then the image of static with black dots frantically swarming the screen came on, for there was nothing being broadcast on that channel. "Well, Your Holiness?" said the King, walking over and sitting back down. "Work your magic"

The Patriarch's staff started glowing brightly until a divine ray of light came from the cross and into the TV's screen. The picture shrunk into blackness as the white noise became silent. Eugenius closed his eyes as the yellow ray dissipated in an instant. Soon, white rings would appear on the screen and become larger until completely vanishing off the screen. The TV would hum louder as more divine power impacted its tubes. The rings became faster until a small image slowly filled the screen, completely hiding the rings, and the humming calmed down as the sound of footsteps would come through the TV's speaker.

The image was angled down onto part of the benches as Parliamentarians, Colonels, and Generals came into the screen's view before sitting down. There was no color in the screen, as the TV was only capable of displaying a black and white picture. Eugenius brought his hands forward to sweep the image downward, resulting in the TV's humming to become louder once more before stopping the image at the wooden podium with the Greek coat of arms and two Greek flags visible in the background. Eugenius let his arms down and opened his eyes, for the TV's humming would turn into silence once more.

Konstantinos arched forward with his snout in his hands while the face of the General blocked out the coat of arms. Chatter could be heard over the speaker as the General waved his hand downward as if to get the attendees to stop their chatter, and the General banged a concealed gavel behind the front podium as the chatter quieted down.

"I have called you all here today to discuss one pressing issue," stated the General. "It seems His Highness, amid all this chaos, has been waist-deep in corruption scandals"

"Should I get the tape recorder?" asked Konstantinos

"I wouldn't think that's necessary," replied Eugenius

"He's been abusing his power to keep the National Union with as many seats as he can get," ranted the General "all the while keeping the Metaxas Party in check."

"If I have permission to speak," said a voice offscreen.

"The motion to speak is now open to all attendees," replied the General.

"I brought this matter before the King—"

"That's His Highness," commented the King gritting his teeth.

"—as Minister of Internal Affairs over the phone since I was over at the U.S. embassy," said the Minister "and he just yelled at me, using profane language. I was lucky that he wanted to schedule another election. I would think that he wouldn't be willing to cooperate in that manner."

Another voice soon chimed in, "With his misuse of public broadcasting funds, it's surprising that they haven't revolted!"

"I've had a word with Konstantinos today," stated Georgios as the King groaned to himself and rubbed his temples behind his horns. "I convinced him to sleep with his blinds open, and when the time comes, we strike!"

"What are you proposing, sir?" asked a voice just offscreen

"I propose that we assassinate the King" said Georgios. "He seemed like he bought it, and it would be an easy task; just have one of our snipers to shoot into that very window and then we could stage our coup."

"But sir, what if he finds out?" asked a voice offscreen

"Well," said the General, "we will discuss that plan when we know that the King and His Holiness are sleeping, and this very precaution will be taken just in case they are watching right this minute."

"But sir," said another voice offscreen. "You certainly don't think they are, do you?"

"Well, with all that we have, we could never be too certain," said the General as hoofbeats could be heard getting closer to the royal chamber. The hoofbeats became louder as the Queen walked in and her gaze turned toward the TV.

"I didn't know that the EIR signed on in the afternoon now," she stated.

"We're not watching TV," explained Konstantinos. "We're watching our Generals conspire to kill us!"

"That's ridiculous," said Anne-Marie, sitting down next to them. "There's no way they actually could be doing something like that."

"It's not the King nor is it the electorate," said Georgios. "It's the idea that people flock behind political parties that's the problem. We could never have a united nation without a united people, and once we kill the king there will be no more 'left' or 'right' There will be only Greeks."

"But sir," said a voice offscreen, "this is a little extreme. There must be some better solutions than to stage a coup like this!"

"Listen," said the General "Greece is like a man with a broken leg. It may well have been an accident that Greece is suffering the way that is. Yet all the nurses keep bickering about petty disagreements and their neighbors. The treatment will be drastic and very painful over a long period of time, but what else are we to do when Dr. Glücksburg forgets the anesthesia all the while opting for older, more ineffective treatment!" The General paused as a murmur of chatter came through the TV speaker.

The Queen was beside herself as her jaw had dropped.

"Now do you see why I've been so worried!" said the King in an angered tone as he stood up, stepped toward the TV, and pressed the volume knob inward, turning it off.

"I-I didn't realize…" stated the Queen as the King sat back down. "We need to do something about this!"

"Wait, wait-wait-wait," said the King "If we call up anyone else, then they'll have an even bigger reason to put a hit on us!"

"It'll happen sooner or later, so why not have the NIS sabotage the General's attempt to overthrow us!" suggested the Queen.

"And cause another civil war?!" exclaimed the King "Last time that happened, we all had to go into hiding in South Africa, and the United States had to invade us!"

"And I wouldn't ever recommend sabotaging Generals like this," said the Patriarch "I tried something similar during Greece's War of Independence against the Ottomans, and the Calif put me under house arrest indefinitely!" exclaimed Eugenius. "Which was the closest thing they could do to execution given my immortality, and I was only let free when the empire fell!"

"Oh," said Anne-Marie. "Well, what should we do instead?"

"If I were you, I'd keep a low profile," said Eugenius, "even if it means never leaving the palace for weeks on end."

A wave of sadness and terror hit them like a tidal wave.

"Well, honey," said Konstantinos. "Looks like we might just be having a good old fashioned home birth."

"If that…" she said as her voice began cracking up.

"There, there," said Konstantinos, bracing Anne-Marie and patting her on the back. "I know this is tough, but we can get through this."

"But what will be Alexia's future when our divine right is cut short?" said the Queen holding back tears.

"Our dynasty survived several revolts and two world wars," eased the King "I'm still Prince of Denmark as well as King of

Greece, so if worse really did come to worse we could hide out at your father's."

"I guess that's true," stated the Queen as Eugenius got up off the couch.

"Sorry to relay the bad news," stated Eugenius. "If you want, I can pray for your survival."

"It's fine," said Konstantinos. "Thank you for your services."

"My pleasure," replied Eugenius before walking out of the chamber shutting the door behind him with a gentle thud.

That night, long after they tucked Alexia in for the night, the Queen walked in and placed her silver crown next to that of her husband's. She undressed and joined her husband in bed.

"Y'know, honey," he said. "I'm a little worried right now."

"You have no reason to fear," said Anne-Marie, rooting through the nightstand for a book to read. "We've shut all the blinds."

"No, no, it's not that," said Konstantinos. "It's that I really worry for the future. With all these nukes, wars, and weather controlling experiments, I wonder if we'll last any longer without creating another apocalypse."

"I know what you mean," stated Anne-Marie. "But if it would make you feel better, I was just wondering what to name our little bundle of joy."

Konstantinos sighed, saying, "I definitely want a nice Greek name."

"Like Callista?" asked Anne-Marie.

"Well," said Konstantinos, "that's assuming that it's a girl"

"When all is said and done, we could always get an ultrasound," said Anne-Marie. "Like we did with Alexia."

"I would rather have it be a surprise this time around," said Konstantinos. "Not like I care either way…y'know? An heir is an heir."

"So what were you thinking if it's a boy?" asked Anne-Marie.

"Something like Gregorios or Pavlos," suggested Konstantinos. "I know my old man would've preferred a Prince over another Princess, but that's because he was old fashioned like that."

Immediately, a black and white furred hand rubbed Konstantinos' muzzle. He looked over toward his wife, who started back at him with a long smile on her face and a book in the other hand.

"Sweetie, you worry too much," she said

"Well, when you have a whole country forced upon you, you end up having to worry about these things," said Konstantinos. "You just chose to be along for the ride."

He turned over in bed and put his own hand beneath Anne-Marie's spotted muzzle, and she giggled in response.

"I loved you the moment we met at my coronation ball," said Konstantinos in a romantic fashion. "You are my prize cow, and you will always be my prize cow, and as the farmer, I will always be there for you."

"Oh ho, Konstantinos, you were always the charmer!" she gleefully replied.

"I aim to please," he said, kissing her.

"Well, good night then," said Anne-Marie as Konstantinos turned off his lamp and went to sleep.

The next morning, Konstantinos woke up as usual, for his wife was still asleep. He got up sitting on the side of the bed and yawned as his right ear perked toward the window, for a low rumbling sound can be heard from outside.

"What the…" he mumbled as he stood up and walked over towards the window, opening the blinds. To his shock and horror, just outside the palace complex walls, there was a cavalcade of drab green tanks rambling past like a flock of dragons. The tanks were accompanied by camo-clad gunmen brandishing assault rifles and machine guns on either side of the flank.

"Honey! Honey!" panicked Konstantinos, shaking Anne-Marie

"Uhh, what is it, Konstantinos?" she said sleepily.

"They've done it! They're surrounding us! Get up, see for yourself!"

Anne-Marie struggled to get out of bed, for she was still half asleep, but seeing the cavalcade was like drinking an espresso shot.

"You need do something!" exclaimed the Queen "Get dressed and talk to them before they blow us sky high!"

"I'll be down there right away, I'll see what this is all about," said Konstantinos, running into the walk-in closet.

Down near the front fence where security guards stood with their weapons drawn in case the Greek troops attack from the front, the tanks might have been out of view, but they still stood ready as the King burst out from the palace entrance with a crooked crown and an open fly. He ran toward the guards, asking in a panicked tone, "Where's General Papadopoulos?"

"Your Highness," said the guard. "It's so good to see you. They're staging a coup, and they want to address you."

"I know that!" exclaimed the King "I saw it from my bedroom; there's no way they'd be using this level of heavy machinery if it was just a coup!"

"Your Highness, that is exactly what the General told me," said the guard as the rumbling became louder. "They want to overthrow you!"

"Let me see for myself," said Konstantinos, opening the palace gate. "Be sure to guard me in case they try something stupid!"

The guards gave a nod in agreement as a tank loomed into view, and General Papadopoulos rode in front of the cavalcade on the back a Centaur soldier wearing full bulletproof armor. Off to the side on the otherwise closed sidewalks were two cameras and microphone booms, for both were in the process of shooting a newsreel.

"HALT!" exclaimed the General, holding his hand out as the tanks stopped and obscured the gates. The cameras zoomed in to the King and the General as the booms moved in closer while still keeping distance.

"Good to see you, Your Highness," said Georgios in a mocking tone. "We have had enough of your corruption and abuse of power. It's time we take the power back into the hands of the people."

"Just so you're aware," fumed the King "you are infringing on my divine right! God gave us the dynasty system, so the public can go on with daily life without having to worry about these things. Almost a hundred years ago, a plebiscite determined that the that the Glücksburgs reign as sovereigns over the Greek people!"

"Your Highness, we are sick and tired of your medieval excuses," said the General before turning back toward the tank. "AIM AND FIRE ON COMMAND!" One of the cameras panned over to the frontmost tank as it moved its cannon toward the direction of the palace with other tanks in the cavalcade following suit. "These shells have been enchanted with fireweed and poison ivy," said the General "If you don't surrender your post as head of state, then your entire palace and all your possessions will all go up in flames, and all that will be left is a giant crater!"

The King looked over to the tanks, thinking about his family, his sculptures, and his music. The guards had their rifles drawn and pointed at the Centaur, who in return pointed his pistol at the guard's head. He gulped and let his head down. "I surrender," he said sheepishly before turning to his guards. "Call a press conference. The public ought to know about this."

"Yes, sir," sighed the guard, walking into the complex beside the palace.

A little while later, there was a mess of microphones topping the podium as cameras were pointed towards it like snipers on a target. There were also several Colonels that stood on either side of the podium and the Hellenic cross adorned the podium. The King got up to the stage and stood up before the podium as he was greeted by a sea of flash bulbs.

"Greece is in a state of stagnation," stated the King resisting to turn toward the generals though his left ear did otherwise. "I have committed a number of misdeeds against the Greek people in the pursuit of freedom from tyranny. My very own Generals have plotted to stage a coup, and their…ferocity in doing so has persuaded me to step down as King of the Hellenes."

He hung his head shamefully as the conference hall was dead silent until a newspaper reporter asked, "Who will be the successor, and what does this mean for Greece at large?"

The King brought his head up and said with a flat face.

"I will entrust my Attorney General, Konstantinos Kallas, as Acting Prime Minister, and if I'm to be frank, I am rather uncertain about the future of this country, but I have faith in my military, as they're specialized in the logistics needed to run this fine nation."

"If you're so concerned about freedom, why are you imposing martial law?" asked another reporter.

"I would prefer not to implement martial law and military rule. They were successful in overthrowing myself and my royal family without any bloodshed. Effective today, I am no longer King of the Hellenes," explained Konstantinos as he took his crown off and placed it on top of the podium. He put his hand on his chest and said, "God bless the people and God bless Greece, may He guide this great nation to its former glory and may He ensure the Greek people freedom from tyranny."

Konstantinos walked out of the conference hall, where Anne-Marie was waiting.

"So, what happened?" she asked.

"We've got to get out of here," said Konstantinos. "I'm only the King in pretense now… Go get Alexia."

"What?" asked Anne-Marie.

"I'm not the King anymore," repeated Konstantinos. "Let's get out of here before the paparazzi finds us!"

"Right," said Anne-Marie. "Which car will we be using?"

"The Opel," answered Konstantinos, "so we don't look suspicious leaving Athens. Now, go get Alexia."

"We'll be there," said Anne-Marie, and just like that, he walked over to the royal garage, and she walked past the palace. The garage featured two ornately designed luxury sedans with one white and the other black, a white sports roadster, a black limousine, and sticking out like a sore thumb was a blue 1953 Opel Olympia. The Opel had large fenders, a waterfall grill, and several large splotches of rust on its paintwork and bumpers, and the front left hubcap was missing. He grabbed Alexia's car seat out of the back of the sedan and flipped the front bench seat downward. He soon put it on the rear seat before pulling the car seat's rear bar over the top of rearmost panel of the car, so it was wedged firmly between the window and the rearmost panel.

He soon unlocked the other door before putting the front bench seat down. Hoofbeats could be heard in the distance.

"Etz go i' bikkar!" announced Alexia.

"Sorry, Alexia, we can't go in the big car," stated Anne-Marie. "We can't afford to do so right now."

"BU' I WANNA GO IBIGKAR!" whined Alexia, stamping her hooves. "I DOWANNA! I DOWANNA!"

Konstantinos promptly gave her a smack on the back.

"Listen!" he boomed, looking down at her. "Daddy was just overthrown, and we can't just drive around in big cars without a bunch of strangers taking pictures or worse. If you don't behave, we won't be going nowhere!"

Alexia started crying before lying down in front of the Ferrari.

"Goodbye, Alexia," said Anne-Marie, walking onto the other side of the Opel.

"Noooo!" said Alexia, running toward Anne-Marie. She grabbed Alexia and placed her into the car seat before Konstantinos flipped the front bench seat back to an upright position. He got his keys out of his left pocket, put them in the ignition, and unlocked the passenger side door, so Anne-Marie could get in. Once he turned the ignition, he steered the car out of the parking space and drove down a ramp, through the Cabinet parking lot down to the guard, which stood before a gate. He rolled down the window, and the guard walked towards him, poking his muzzle through the window.

"I can't let you through!" said the guard "Certainly not without alerting Prime Minister Kollas!"

"Listen, I need to keep this quiet," explained Konstantinos. "We're going into hiding in the Tatoi palace, and no one should be able to see us"

The guard nodded before walking back and pressing a few buttons. The gate opened, and Konstantinos drove past the gate and onto the relatively vacant street. "Ugh, how do my subjects drive these things?" complained Konstantinos, noting the car's lack of power steering.

"You were the one who wanted to look inconspicuous," reminded Anne-Marie.

Konstantinos immediately rolled the window up at the first stop sign as Alexia asked, "Pay meusic?"

Konstantinos looked down at the dash and said, "There isn't a tape player in here, but there is a radio," before pressing its 'MW' button, causing it to crack into life.

"This date, the 21st of April, 1967, will go down in history as the start of a new era!" said a voice over the speaker. "An era for Greece and Europe at large. An era of freedom and peace, of wealth and prosperity, and of a new Greece. The phoenix has risen from the ashes of party politics. No more Metaxas; no more National Union, for there will be only Greeks under one junta and one regime from here on out! It is I, Attorney General and Prime Minister Kallas, who will place the cast on this ailing nation, and I shall ensure that no family will ever starve to death or be divided on opinion. I will turn this country around, and I will correct all of the unjust that the Glücksburg dynasty has wrought over the past century!"

Thunderous applause played over the speaker in response to the Attorney General's speech as Konstantinos changed the station to one that was playing music.

"Oh, sweetie," said Anne-Marie, worried. "What will we do now?"

"Looks like we'll just live like regular citizens in Tatoi until I think of something," said Konstantinos.

"Me Princess?" asked Alexia

"I don't know," stated Konstantinos. "I just don't know anymore."

They drove through suburbs and houses as they cruised down the highway away from the palace they once ruled in. Not too long after, the urban splendor of Athens turned into many small fields and shanty houses. The ride became bumpy, as the road was now made of dirt. Rusty cars could be seen being driven down some nearby dirt roads. The car was near silent as the gravity of the situation had hit them like an 18-wheeler.

After a while, they turned off on a road that led into a cypress forest as more homes passed them by. Next, they turned toward a dirt road that made the car rattle and shake until they reached the elaborate Tatoi palace that was tucked away in national park land and far away from the eyes of the prying public.

"We're here," sighed Konstantinos, turning off the car and opening the door to get out.

"Are we really going to spend the rest of our lives out here?" asked Anne-Marie, getting out of the car as well.

"There's still the NIS," shrugged Konstantinos before he proceeded to flip the front bench seat down "They're the only people who haven't tried to kill us, and I can only hope that we won't have our kid out here!"

"Wi 'i be boy 'o girl?" Asked Alexia as Anne-Marie soon got her out of the car seat.

"I don't know, sweetie," consoled Anne-Marie. "But sometimes, it's just better to not know"

"Why, Mommy?" asked Alexia as her mother undid her car seat and proceeded to carry it

"Well, there's a lot of things I know that make me and Daddy sad," said Anne-Marie. "It's not only the good things we know; it's the really bad stuff we have to know, too, and there's more bad than good in the world."

"Why, Mommy?" asked Alexia as they walked up the stairs up to the palace.

"I don't know," replied Anne-Marie as they walked behind Konstantinos. "But you're going to like being out here."

"On trip?" asked Alexia as Konstantinos got his key out of his pocket and put it in the palace's keyhole.

"I wish," sighed Konstantinos, unlocking the door. "I really wish this was just a trip." He opened the front door solemnly, revealing the palace's large windows and several lamps. It was nowhere near as elaborate as the one in Athens. It still had all the luxury and splendor with many portraits, landscapes, and other golden appointments throughout.

"Where TB?" asked Alexia, noticing only a console stereo in the center of the room with a Victorian-style couch facing toward it.

"Not everywhere has TV," explained Konstantinos, squatting down to her level as she began to cry.

"Bu I wa—TB!" whined Alexia as her voice broke up, and she sobbed on the palace carpet.

"Now, I know it's tough being away from home," said Konstantinos, patting her on the back. "But I'm gonna tell you the truth. Daddy is in big trouble, and we need to be here until I can correct what I've done."

"Ca—say surry?" Asked Alexia once she was lifted by her mother and stopped crying.

"I'm afraid it's not that simple with grown-ups," explained Konstantinos, "especially when they wanted Daddy to die! But don't worry, we'll be able to go back before you know it." He gave her a pat on the back before she and her mother walked upstairs to inspect the bedroom. A tear fell down the side of his face. He sat down on the couch as snot oozed from his nostrils.

He wiped the tears away with a handkerchief as his tail migrated between the couch cushions, and he sat, staring at the stereo as a sign of things to come.

A few weeks later, the royal family remained in hiding. Konstantinos could be seen sitting on the living room couch with Anne-Marie. They both had mangy matted fur while they listened to the radio. His maw was in his hand, and her brow was scrunched in anger as they listened to a propaganda ad.

"Dooii, I don't buy Greek made wine because the workers aren't free to choose," said a retarded-sounding version of the King "Don't be King Careless. Always trust goods approved by the junta," rebuked a stern sounding announcer.

The announcer kept talking as a knocking was heard on Konstantinos' door. He rubbed his eyes and got up.

"I'll get it," he said tiredly, getting up and walking toward the door. He opened it, revealing a rather familiar dark-haired Human with a clipboard in hand. "Elias!" he said with a smile on his face. "What have you got for us now!"

"Your ex-guard has brought more groceries, Your Highness," he replied. "And we've also brought news from the Capitol."

"Have they cancelled the auction?" Konstantinos asked hopefully.

"No, Your Highness," sighed Elias as he walked into the palace. "But I'm here to show you the new flag of Greece."

"I heard they were changing it," Konstantinos said, following the former head of the NIS, "but I didn't know what it looked like."

Elias got out a small flag from his pocket that had nine white stripes and a white cross on the top left corner with a midnight blue background. Konstantinos looked at it and cringed.

"I figured they were gonna get rid of the crown, but I didn't know they'd outright go for the naval ensign!"

"Well, Your Highness, it is the military after all," stated Elias humbly, sitting on the couch.

"They never had any business with the navy though!" exclaimed Konstantinos, sitting down with him. "Isn't that right, hun?"

Elias proceeded to hand Anne-Marie the flag as she grabbed it with her left hand.

"I mean, we have plenty of islands," she said, rubbing her distended belly with her right, "but more people live on the mainland than any of the isles put together!"

"Wait till you see the new coat of arms," said Elias, getting a copy of the coat of arms off the clip board and holding it up. The coat of arms consisted of a pictogram of a phoenix rising out of flames.

"What the hell is that flaming bird supposed to mean for the country!" exclaimed Anne-Marie.

"They say that it has to do with renewal for the country," explained Elias. "It doesn't make sense to me either, but that's how they explained it."

"The only thing I think they're renewing is the might of Spartan warriors with a coat of arms like that!" said Konstantinos bitterly while pouting. "I mean, those tyrants might as well be sacrificing bulls to Zeus at this rate!"

"And now we return to the Greek palace charity auction, live from Athens…" said the announcer as the room went silent. Chatter would come over the speakers before the voice of General Papadopoulos boomed through the faint sound of radio static.

"I'm pleased to announce the start of this charity auction," said the General cordially as the chatter died down "To crack down on old partyism and to assist those who are unfortunate, I've brought it upon myself to auction off old royal possessions because nothing should be part of one family anymore."

"Yes, because everything should belong to the grand pubaa of the army!" remarked Konstantinos sarcastically.

"So let's start off with our experienced auctioneer," said Georgios. "Take it away."

A couple subtle footsteps and hoofbeats could be heard from the speakers before the voice of the auctioneer came on.

"Thank you very much, sir, and now we're gonna start with lot 323 with this compact cassette recorder," said the auctioneer. "This tape recorder is the smallest in the world. It can fit in a shoebox, and the tape is already wound together in one neat, removable plastic cartridge. It's fully transistorized with no need for threading and can record for up to two hours on one cartridge. Perfect for home, office, and royal spying on phone calls."

"The Americans do it, too, Einstein," complained Elias. "It's called security."

"The bidding will start at 300 drachmae," he announced before rattling off all the bids in rapid succession.

"We need to put a stop to this!" exclaimed Anne-Marie as the bids piled up.

"Honey, if we did that," said Konstantinos, "they'd sic a firing squad on us. There's a reason we still live here!"

Anne-Marie gulped as the auctioneer announced, "Twenty-five hundred...going once... 2,500 going twice... SOLD for 2,500 drachmae to bidder number 19. Come on up here and claim your tape recorder."

"I swear he's doing this to spite me!" complained Konstantinos.

"With all of his propaganda posters, are you really surprised?" asked Elias as footsteps followed by the sound of rolling wheels could be heard over the speakers.

"I guess not," said Konstantinos.

"Next is lot 607," the auctioneer said. "An ancient marble sculpture of the Greek god Apollo, dated 251 BC, untarnished by iconoclastic vandals; it makes a fascinating edition to gardens, witch covens, and private collections."

"Oh, not the sculptures," cringed Konstantinos, reaching his hands behind his horns to rub his temples. "Those are royal heirlooms!"

"The bidding will start at 40,000 drachmae," announced the auctioneer before rattling off all the new bids.

"Don't worry," said Anne-Marie. "We can always find other sculptures."

"Not ancient ones though!" complained Konstantinos. "I mean, imagine if the Danish military was auctioning off untarnished rune stones or Viking tapestries! Those are priceless historical artifacts!"

"Four-hundred-thousand going once...400,000 going twice..." announced the auctioneer. "Five-hundred-thousand! Now, the bid is 500,000 drachmae. Six-hundred...where? Six-hundred… the bid still stands at 500,000, five, five five, 500,000 going once…500,000 going twice… SOLD for 500,000 drachmae to bidder 23."

"I really want to give them a piece of my mind right now, but it's just so hard, y'know!" exclaimed Konstantinos.

"It's okay," said Anne-Marie, patting her husband's hand. "We'll get out of here if things get bad."

"Next is lot 112," announced the auctioneer as more footsteps and rolling was heard over the speakers. "This 65 cm TV is a state secret no longer. It has handsome, modern styling, a 13-channel tuner, brightness and contrast controls, and a rooftop antenna for the best possible picture quality."

"They can't be serious," complained Konstantinos. "I had to import that from West Germany!"

"I remember," said Anne-Marie. "That was such a nice gesture, too."

"I wanted to put Greece into the twentieth century through television!" exclaimed Konstantinos furiously. "If it weren't for me, they'd all be stuck in the dark ages!"

"It's just like radio," explained the auctioneer, "but with images as well as sound, perfect for relaxing at home while being informed and entertained by our channels, the EIR and the AFS as well as telling fortunes and spying on your enemies!"

Konstantinos promptly got up when the auctioneer began rattling off all the bids. He walked into the kitchen towards a green rotary phone, where he carefully but swiftly navigated the rotor towards a small wedge-shaped metal piece and let it go, so it could be returned for dialing the next number in sequence. Once the process was complete, he picked up the handle and waited for someone to answer. At first, all that came through was a dial tone.

"Hello?" answered a familiar voice once the dial tone stopped.

"Michalis," smiled Konstantinos. "Did you hear about the auction?"

"Yes, I did," said the guard. "It's ridiculous."

"Well, I have a plan to stop the regime's nonsense," he said

"Are you going to the auction to intervene, or what are we doing?" asked Michalis.

"It's not just the auction," explained Konstantinos. "It's the whole junta that overthrew me. I say we gather up a faction of royalists and stage a counter-coup!"

"You can't be serious," said Michalis

"So long as that blasted bird is Greece's new symbol, my birthright is in jeopardy!" exclaimed Konstantinos. "We need a royalist force behind us, so we can shoot out every one of those goddamn paratroopers."

"But Your Highness," he said. "What if we shoot out a bunch of innocents?"

"We just have to aim carefully," stated Konstantinos. "But in any event, I'm not going to sit here while those fucking Colonels turn Greece into a dystopian hellscape!"

"Of course, Your Highness," replied Michalis. "I'll rally the opposition."

"Perfect," said Konstantinos. "With our numbers, I'll be sure to take back what's mine!"

"We'll be there in a couple of hours," stated Michalis. "See you then, Your Highness."

"You too," replied Konstantinos as he proceeded to hang up and walk back into the living room.

"What did he say?" asked Elias.

"They're going to be here in a few hours while they rally the troops," explained Konstantinos.

"Well, that's good news," commented Anne-Marie

"Four thousand going once…4,000 going twice…" announced the auctioneer before an audible strike of the gavel. "SOLD for 4,000 drachmae to bidder number 65, come on up here and claim your tele—" There was a crack and a click before Konstantinos turned off the radio, and all was silent thereafter.

A little while after the clock struck three, the counter-coup resistance showed up to the cobblestone driveway in sedans, vans, and pickup trucks. The three came out to see what was the noise, only to find a haphazard cavalcade sitting before them.

"Are you ready, Your Highness?" asked one of the guards.

"Did you bring arms?" he asked.

"Of course, Your Highness. It wouldn't be a counter coup without them," said the guard as he brandished a machine gun.

"Nikolas, get the Opel, so you can lead the charge," ordered Konstantinos.

"Yes, sir," replied Nikolas before he walked toward the garage.

"I wish you he best of—" Anne-Marie began but was interrupted by an intense pain in her belly. "Oh! The baby is coming!" she exclaimed

"Oh, that's great, hun" he said, forcing a smile. "Mehmet, could you kindly take my wife to the bedroom and help deliver the baby?"

"Yes, Your Highness," replied Mehmet as Anne-Marie gritted her teeth in pain. She was slowly escorted back into the palace.

Later, Konstantinos got in the back seat of the Mercedes sedan where a machine gun and several enchanted ammo cartridges were placed. He turned on the walkie talkie and said, "I'm in the nest 1-0-2," in code.

"10-4 on the Olympic syndicate," replied a soldier on the walkie talkie.

"Run through the seagulls and put them in the freezer, over," said Konstantinos.

"Copy that," replied another driver. "The bats will fly through the roots and ice the seagulls."

Radio chatter stopped as the cavalcade worked their way out of the driveway and out onto the dirt highways out of the woods. They got out onto a paved road that led right into Athens.

"Branch out, and ice the seagulls," said Konstantinos into the walkie talkie.

"Copy that, 1-0-2," replied one of the soldiers as a looming sight came over the city skyline. An orange smoldering phoenix was seen in the sky hurling fireballs and magma feathers onto the streets below.

"The roots are full of bats!" exclaimed the soldier "Repeat, the roots are full of bats! Spread out and Ice the seagulls"

The calvalcade scrambled down different streets before Konstantinos rolled down the window as he said, "Nikolas, turn on the reel-to-reel tape player. I'd like some music for the occasion."

"My pleasure," replied the driver before he turned on the tape player and rock music bellowed out of the car speakers. He pointed his gun out the window and shot at every paratrooper he could see. They were frozen in place as the bullet's magic induced frostbite and reduced their legs to glasslike stubs.

The driver would power slide around large turns and molten sections of road as Konstantinos would get flung back, so he laid down on the bench seat. His right horn got chipped on the other door as he sat back upright and yelled out, "What do you think of this, fascistic scum!" before opening fire on more cops. Sirens could be heard in the distance, as they were soon pursued by two cop cars. "Step on it, Nikolas. I can't be King from jail!"

"Yes, Your Highness," replied Nikolas, getting the car into high gear as officers would shoot out at his car. Konstantinos shot back, breaking their windshield and freezing their faces in place. The ice spread as the police cruiser raced at high speeds before their heads rolled off their bodies, and they crashed into a hardware store. The rest of the cavalcade would meet back up as they raced past apartments and cafes at 110 km/h, skidding across turns and streets like giant hockey pucks being struck by sticks.

The palace approached quickly before some of the troops drove headfirst into the fenced perimeter, a couple even crashing into the Guard's bunks.

"Nikolas, get us up to the gate, so our counter-coup will be known throughout history!"

"Yes, Your Highness," replied Nikolas as he and the other drivers slowed down in front of the gate and stopped. Once they turned off their cars, they got up to the guards and shot them with flaming bullets before they could react. Their togas caught fire as other soldiers shot their darkness bullets wildly, hitting any remaining guards, killing them before they rapidly decomposed into skeletons in their uniforms.

Konstantinos and his entourage ran into his gutted palace down the halls and toward the staircase. Two of his old statues jaunted toward the staircase and smacked the soldiers upside the head. The soldiers quickly had the wind knocked out of them before the statues quickly handcuffed them and laid them in Konstantinos' way.

He tripped on them for they lie on the second stair from the top before he fell on solid marble, landing face first. Just as he tried getting up, the guard's Senior Officers opened the door and blocked the exit. They promptly drew their uzis and pointed them at the disposed King. Other Senior Officers blocked the upper stairwell along with General Papadopoulos.

Taking a few breaths, the General stepped down to the second level looking down upon Konstantinos while blood dripped from his severely bruised nose. The soldiers wriggled against the marble statues' grip to no avail.

"It's no use doing anything else. You fell right into my trap," said the general.

Konstantinos was at a loss for words.

"I sold off all that wasn't useful to us" explained the General "But why pay guards when you can turn these sculptures into Golems, You might just recognize one of them from your old coat of arms."

Tense, Konstantinos got up and turned around to see the statue to his right was of Zeus and the one to his left was all too familiar "Heracles!" he exclaimed in surprise as the statues stood stoically "Bu-how?"

"Such a waste of Heraldry" said the General in a condescending tone "You rather boost your ego than to bolster your own defense. They never need food, nourishment or rest and they're a part of the nation's history at that. All it took was to get you to dispose of your own guard and I can lap it up in the papers."

"You w-won't get away with this," rebuked Konstantinos, wincing in pain as his tie was now stained with blood.

"Oh, King Careless," grinned the general to himself, "always so retrograde."

"What's retrograde is getting heraldic slaves to do one's bidding," groaned Konstantinos as he pointed the gun at the General's chest. "This is for God, Country & family!" He pulled the trigger, but there was only a metallic click as it wasn't loaded.

"I could've been your Regent, but you chose to disregard the Greeks," said the General with a sly grin "Men, take these old partyists away to the national prison!"

The statues quickly lifted the bodies and walked off with them without saying a word.

"You'll be remembered as a tyrant," said Konstantinos. "The madman who imprisoned the rightful holder of the throne."

"Oh no, I'm not putting you in prison," said the General "I've got something special planned for you…"

Anne-Marie had a boy that day as Konstantinos was subsequently stripped of his Greek citizenship and deported to Italy along with the rest of the family. Greece hasn't had a King since, closing the book on thousands of years of monarchical rule in the country. The junta would be disestablished seven years later, and they all lived happily sometimes after…

The End

4
CURSED

I can still remember it like it was yesterday; I parked my car on a large and busy street in the small Florida city of Fort Walton Beach. It was my hometown and I knew the area real well.

"LIQUIDATION SALE, EVERYTHING MUST GO," read the front window of a local clothes boutique.

I normally avoided going into boutiques like this due to the expensive prices on garments and my limited pocketbook. This time, however, I didn't think anything of it, it was just a fast, cheap way to pass the time. I entered the establishment, and inside was nearly barren with coat racks and dress racks with little clothing on them. I noticed only two other people inside—the cashier and a man that I could only presume was buying something. I walked over toward the righthand side of the shop toward the dress rack. Most of the dresses were 1940s vintage dresses with plain colors and simple patterning around the midsection.

One in particular caught my eye: a blue and white plaid dress ensemble complete with a thin, black leather belt. *Seems a little tacky...* I thought, not usually being one to go for vintage clothing like this *But for 90 cents what could go wrong.* I unhooked the dress's hanger from the rack as the other customer left.

"Can I help you?" asked the cashier, who now looked in my direction. The cashier was a young and thin looking, dark brown skinned woman with dark, wavy hair.

I looked over to her and said, "Uhh, yeah, I like this dress, but I'm not sure if it'll look good on me…"

The cashier stared at me funny before she said with this big 'ol grin, "It'll just be perfect. Follow me to the dressing room and try it on!"

I then followed her toward an arch with a large, navy-blue curtain in the back, lefthand corner of the shop. The cashier would pull back the curtain to reveal a mirror, a wooden stand-up coat hanger as well as a tall metal studio lamp for illumination.

"Are you sure this is right for me?" I asked one last time.

"Don't worry," said the cashier as she put the dress on the hanger. "I know my clothes, and you will fit just perfectly. And if you don't like it, I'll just put it back on the shelf."

Reassured, I went into the dressing room as the cashier turned the lamp on. I pulled the curtain behind me and put down my tan leather purse while the lamp gave off this aweful orange haze to my reflection.

I examined myself in the mirror. In those days I was a decent lookin' brunette, but not like a supermodel or anything. I looked at the ensemble that I was wearing already: loose brown slacks, a plain purple blouse with a white overcoat, and blue sneakers. I never cared much about fashion then, come to think of it, this was the last time I went out without makeup. I probably needed it too since I had these pimples at the time and this messy brown hairstyle. I started off by taking off my overcoat and putting it on the coat hanger just below where I put the dress.

I turned back towards the mirror to take my shirt off and placed it on the ground, revealing a pair of braless, B-cup breasts.

I took my shoes off by untying them and pulling them off, which made taking my pants off much easier. I pulled my pants down to my ankles before I stepped out of them. I looked at my pale, nearly naked body in the mirror before I turned towards the hanger to try on the dress. I tossed the belt to the ground before I looked at the dress itself. It was a single piece that was around 3ft. long from the collar down to the end; this made it easy to slip over my body until the blouse portion.

I slid it back over my head and flipped it back over to the front end to find that every button on the blouse portion was still fastened.

Having discovered this, I took it off and unbuttoned every button to try once more to put the dress on. Once again, I was successful in putting the dress on until the blouse portion, as it was still a little tight as it went over my boobs. In hindsight I suspect it was intentional but once the cinched part of the blouse portion had passed it, the dress became much comfier. Finally, I put my arms through the short but slightly puffed-out sleeves. I reached down for the belt and put it with my other clothes, I mean, the dress seemed to fit me fine enough.

It was only then, I discovered one problem with the dress: the sleeves were just a little bit too small for my upper arms.

"It doesn't fit," I said, but there was only silence, no reply— just silence. "Hello?" I said, turning around as the silence weirded me out. I pulled back the curtain only to find that there was no one there. "Where did she go?" I wondered aloud, scanning the store.

Now, I was the only one in the store with only the occasional sound of passing cars and footsteps that broke the silence. I spotted something that was missing from the front window, and just before I stepped to investigate, I felt like this binding energy squeezing down on my whole body. I tried to move, but my muscles wouldn't cooperate, not even so much as to close my mouth or move my eyes around. I was terrified and I wanted to scream, but I couldn't.

From the back, I heard footsteps that were getting progressively louder. It moved and curved around me until I saw who those footsteps belonged to. The cashier presented herself before my line of sight, and said with a knowing smile.

"I told you it would be perfect! Now, just to pose you…"

P-pose! I mentally exclaimed as the cashier began moving my arms into place. I felt her palms working my arms in an outward going position and my hands into an open and upwards position. She squatted down to examine my legs, as the dress went down below my knees, leaving my ankles exposed.

"A bit too hairy… But I don't think I'll be needin' the legs."

HAIRY! I thought as I still couldn't speak. *Pardon me for not being a dainty little barbie doll!*

She got up and closed my mouth before manipulating my face into a subtle grin.

HELP ME! I wanted to cry out, but my mouth was still shut, and people walked past the boutique as if nothing was happening. The cashier moved behind me, and her footsteps became quieter before stopping. I was left to smile in fear until the footsteps became louder. The cashier came back with the belt in hand and proceeded to wrap it around my midsection below my belly button before she securely fastened it through the third to last belt loop.

What the fuck is going on! I wondered as the cashier's footsteps became progressively quieter to the point of vanishing. I wanted to escape and walk out of the boutique so bad, but I still remained just standing in a pose with my eyes fixed toward the window and the street scenery.

Footsteps came back after a few minutes, and they became louder until the cashier presented herself to me again, but this time, she was holding a strange wooden staff with a hog's skull that adorned the top if it.

What the, what are you doing? I thought as this red magic filled the inside of the hog's skull, and the cashier began chanting in a weird language. The red magic inside the hog's skull became ever brighter until the apparent Voodoo sorceress aimed the red energy at my chest. I was overwhelmed by all that was happening, and I wanted to scream for help, but my face was stuck in a content smirk

The magic hurt a lot, it felt like this very intense stinging like someone put my whole body in acid. It hurt to the point where if I wasn't bewitched, I'd have been screaming in pain. I felt like I was dying and I even wondered if this is what it felt like to die. But it all became apparent once the red magic stopped firing; my chest area felt numb and strange while I felt intense chest pains like I was havin' a heart attack. The pulsating chest pains became strangely numbed out in a matter of seconds, yet the pain kept migrating down my midsection. I couldn't move or call for an ambulance, and all I could do was die as the pulsing sensation of my entrails waned away and vanished completely.

Just when I thought the pains had stopped, my legs began to atrophy yet solidify. My legs lost any form that they once possessed, until they became two large metallic sticks. I heard my socks rip into shreds even though the area was completely numb as my feet rounded out into nearly-perfect semi-circles before merging together to create one chrome circle on the floor. What was left of my legs moved towards the center of the circle and merged into, like, this pole.

What was once my ass and vagina lost definition and folded downwards beneath my midsection until it was a clean, seamless stub. I then felt this tunneling sensation at the base of my torso as my pole screwed itself into my now-hollow midsection. I mentally screamed in pain once more because my arms had dislocated into seams beneath the sleeves of the dress. The same acidic stinging pain and dislocation was repeated through my elbows and wrists. Finally, my neck slightly dislocated into a seam as stinging and numbing permeated my mouth and braincase until there was nothing.

I was in no pain, and I didn't feel anything in spite of wearing a dress that didn't fit perfectly in the arms. The cashier watched my changes, but I didn't pay any attention to her until she walked up to me and spun me around, so I was now looking in the direction of the dressing room I just got out of. I didn't feel her hands or the pressure of them pushing on my body; Yet, I was like, aware. That was kind of the weird part, I saw and heard everything that happened to me. The cashier opened the curtain with her right hand while she held onto the staff with her left. It revealed something shocking and horrible.

I was now nothing more than a plastic display mannequin on a reflective chrome base; my eyes and mouth were now strokes of paint, and my once messy brown hair was now a perfectly straight wig as if it were crafted from horsehair. I wanted to cry, but I didn't have any tears. Yeah I was poor, but at the same time, my entire life was ahead of me; I was a college sophomore at Northwest Florida State College and I was studying to be a psychologist; I moved out of my house at 18 and I had a part-time job as a waitress at an Italian restaurant; and worst yet, my first boyfriend, Anthony was to meet me in an hour at the nearby Fort Walton Beach public library to tutor me in Spanish.

While I was unscrewed from my stand and effortlessly carried to the back, I couldn't help but think about all the minor pleasures of life that I would miss, things like: driving, watching TV at home, making phone calls, grocery shopping, and simply managing to complete the Fall 1980 semester. I had many sad thoughts whirling around my empty hollow head as I was put in a large shipping crate bound for somewhere I couldn't see. The crate contained several other mannequins wearing clothes, so it seemed at least that I wasn't the first.

>─┤◆〉─◆─Ο─◆〈◆─┤─<

I quickly lost track of time since that Voodoo witch turned me into a mannequin and put me in the crate. I was entirely numb, yet I didn't even feel like an inanimate object anymore. In this state, I felt oddly Human as I began seeing these vivid. I don't know what exactly to call them, Visions? Dreams? But, anyways, I found myself sitting in a well-furnished room with a TV showing something and a lamp that kinda rippled and flexed as it changed color.

The leather couch remained beige as I took gulps out of a soda can without even tasting the fluid contained within. Stranger still, my great grandad suddenly appeared sitting on the opposite end of the couch. Now, this was alarming and confusing. He'd been dead for a few years at the time and I actually went to his funeral when I was 14!

A number of possibilities and questions had come up in my mind.

Now, I'd read about how people in extreme isolation hallucinate, be it mirages in the desert or former Alcatraz inmates who spent time in solitary confinement. But everything seemed too vivid and real for anything like that.

Then, I figured I was dead, and this was purgatory. I didn't know how painful that transformation was, so maybe it was so much pain that it killed me.

I eliminated that possibility because I hadn't seen any sign of Angels or heard the voice of God as the Minister at my old church had informed me, I would.

Then I thought that this was all a very vivid nightmare; after all I'd read in the papers about a witch who put curses in cheese to abuse her own son through nightmares.

But last time I checked, the fridge was possibly out of cheese, and there wouldn't be anyone in my life with that kind of vendetta.

I then heard the abrupt sound of footsteps, some faint rolling noises and the faint words, "This place gives me the creeps."

And another faint voice: "Yeah, but we've got a job that needs doin'."

The footsteps marched back and forth while the voices followed suit. Reality just blanked out before it became a brick stairwell that grew taller with each footstep I heard.

I climbed the stairs as I could just make out phrases such as, "Those ones have clothes in 'em," and "Don't forget all them filing cabinets," but I kept goin' up the stairs as the changing colors calmed down to a cool brown as the width of the stairs narrowed. A grunting noise could be heard along with the footsteps and rolling. All the noises became louder in my left ear and vanished out my right.

I finally got to the top of the stairs, where there was a building that looked like the library where I met my tutor and boyfriend. The building was brick like the stairwell, and I had no choice but to enter as I heard more rolling going on in my right ear and grunting coming out of my left. This library looked weird and blurry with no posters or even a librarian, but I did see these see these ghost Angels walking in by phasing through the walls.

I went down each aisle looking at tiles while the footsteps and rolling were the loudest they've been yet!

"Shh!" I said before the entire library tilted up at a 30-degree angle. *Knock!* I heard as my surroundings went back to total darkness. I could practically hear grunting right behind me and I wanted to scream *HELP! THERE'S A MONSTER NEARBY!* But now, everything was in focus, I couldn't talk, nor did I have the means to talk in the first place.

Turned out I really was going crazy because of isolation, and worse still was the realization that I was indeed, a plastic dummy, presumably being transported God knows where. This presumption was backed up by the loud rumbling sound of a truck, but before I could think about it, I was tilted back even more before the crate became right side up again.

I lie down flat as I heard a series of loud metallic clangs before the truck's engine became significantly muted.

The police better find me! I thought helplessly. *I might have been broken by these goons!*

What! I said as the crate began to vibrate. *I'm not some prissy little doll, what the hell am I thinking?* Reality set in as I painlessly hit my head on the side of the crate, and I remembered the fact that I haven't been hungry or sleepy during my bout of whatever it was.

There were no more hallucinations save for a few stray colors for hours on end. I slid and bounced with each instance of traffic on top of the droning sound of the truck's motor while I waited to see light. I'd have been in the dark for who knows how long, and the jerkiness of traffic wasn't doing any favors.

At least I don't have a stomach anymore… I thought to myself gratefully.

The truck motor stopped

Here at last, I thought with great relief before I heard the glorious sound of metal doors opening, then I heard a few more metallic clanging noises. *Please don't break me,* I thought, not knowing how durable I was. I was tilted backwards and I could only presume that I was being moved elsewhere.

"This contains the mannequins from Florida, right?" I heard upon the crate being leveled.

"Yes, madame, of course," replied the movers.

"Good, now get the other things."

"Yes, madame."

The sound of footsteps vanished into the distance before I heard some wooden creaking noises, some more distant sounding than others.

I was grabbed by the torso while I was blinded by the white glow of the surrounding fluorescent lamps before I was turned around to face an old woman with a sagging, dark brown face who looked at me with a slight grin.

"I have something great stored for you," said the old woman holding me. "In just a few minutes, you will be forever beautiful."

She walked into another room holding me in her arms, and I was kind of distraught. I hated the prissy popular girls who obsessed over body image— I'd been bullied by them all through high school after all. But I digress, I was college student with a job and career goals! I was ballistic as my head was twisted off like a screw being driven out. Next, I was set down facing away from the mirror and toward what looked like a coffee maker and a stack of books on chemistry and witchcraft.

She walked out with my torso and arms, leaving me as a disembodied head. It was official for me, I figured that if I could survive beheading, maybe becoming a mannequin wasn't so bad after all. Come to think of it, there's times even now I miss being a mannequin, I mean we struggle with sustaining a body so we can live; so, when you don't have to sustain anything because you're immortal plastic, all you can do is exist and be cared for.

At the time though, I figured that if the police did find me, they could always turn me back to normal later on. After all, these people were probably doing something shady with the rest of my body. I heard footsteps coming back followed by the sound of something being let down. I was lifted up off the table and screwed onto a different body as the world around me spun around before it stopped.

I could see myself in the mirror while the body was dressed in high heels, black nylon leggings, and a red and white striped bra. My face was content and topped with medium-length brown hair; my hips were wide and well-toned, and my breasts were and still are 33 DD, so whoever had this body last was someone who I definitely figured frequented the gym.

I couldn't help, but admire my overall form.

Oh, the guys I could attract this if all this were Human... I thought wistfully as the lady called toward the hall: "Hey Lisa, what do y'all think?"

I heard other footsteps and some muttering until I saw a very familiar face come in from behind the mirror. It was the face of the very witch who duped me.

"Oh, I think she looks gorgeous," she said. "Absolutely perfect for the window!"

"Gorgeous..." and "perfect..." echoed around my head as the two witches continued to talk. *Why have I missed out on looking this sexy for so long?* I wondered. *It's a blessing that I finally get to be perfect.*

No longer would I struggle to get anywhere as I was carried from the room to the front of the store. No longer would I have to worry about making ends meet, as money almost seemed ridiculous now. No longer would I even be concerned with a career of any kind as I was mounted to the front window display

I looked out over the vacant strip mall parking lot as the sun rose.

I felt that this was my purpose, and sole purpose: looking pretty for the customers all the while serving as a living advertisement for the clothes on offer at this store.

Here I was, standing still and stagnant as a mannequin in a clothing shop window. All I could see was the parking lot loaded with coupes and station wagons while cars moved up and down a single lane road with a series of houses on the opposite end of the store. The hours passed by as I saw a variety of faces going in and out of the store until I heard a conversation among the store's music.

"Hey girl," greeted a customer to the cashier.

"Hey, how have you been? I haven't seen y'all in ages," replied the cashier.

"Oh things have been good, I dun broke up with my boyfriend, but I'm long over him. So I see that things didn't work out in Florida?" asked the customer.

"Things began slowing down, and I couldn't make any money, so I moved back here to help out my sister," replied the cashier before they moved closer to me.

"So, you two finally got that mannequin for the other window," remarked the customer.

"Isn't she beautiful?" said the cashier. "I got her while I was in Florida, but now she's the belle of St. Mary parish."

PARISH! I thought. *But, there's only one place in the world that has parishes!* I remembered a conversation I had with a classmate a year prior. *I'm in Louisiana!* I panicked as they continued talking and laughing behind me. The customer bought her things before I saw her walk out of the store and away from my line of sight.

I didn't know what to think. On one hand, I assumed that I'd more than likely never see my folks again, but on the other hand, the old life was no more. These thoughts whirled around my little head for the rest of the day as cars came and went. Big downside to being a mannequin though is that life is awfully boring with no school or relationships to make things more varied and your owners have to protect you from getting so much as a scratch.

By nightfall, the store closed, and everyone walked away while leaving me behind in the dark.

There was no moon in the sky, and I could only see a couple houses with lights on and streetlights that served to illuminate the grey sidewalk. I was very much left in the dark, abandoned for hours on end until the morning people opened the door and readied the registers for the day's work. More cars pulled up, and customers walked in and out of the shop while conversations about sizes drifed all around my ears.

Several days passed before I was screwed off my mount and carried into the back. From there, the bra and high-heeled shoes were taken off, immediately followed by the leggings. I didn't feel a thing as many hands touched me. I wasn't aroused nor frightened anymore, for it was just natural for a doll like me. Just like how my legs and arms were screwed off my torso followed by my head—Dismemberment was just another painless part of my weekly routine.

I could hear them fumbling around with my body parts, but all I wanted to do was to be whole, I was never a fan of just being a head. Twenty minutes later, they picked my head up and screwed it onto my otherwise assembled body. In the mirror, I noticed myself wearing green heels and a pair of blue jeans that served to complement my plump ass with a striped tee on my torso. I looked marvelous in 70's casual, and I was carried to my display window, where I noticed a handsome doll in the other window. I wasn't really bothered to make out details, but he seemed to have been made into the perfect man. I was put in my window and fastened to my stand for another week of being on display.

That was my weekly routine: I stood in the window before my owner's staff came to dress me up in another outfit. No matter if it was antebellum or vintage or even trendy postmodern, I'd always look beautiful. I mean, my parts were selected to be the very embodiment of beauty. I felt I could help my owners sell clothes or even get rich in the process. I grew to love being owned, as it was my entire life purpose, and I figured I would always serve as a dummy. I remember watching all those humans coming and driving and walking. I thought about how they worried and feared about goals, but I never needed to worry; I had owners to worry for me.

All I needed to do was to be beautiful.

Months turned into years and I learned all sorts of wonderful things about my owners. Like how they were around 270 years old and used mortal limbs to make themselves more powerful. My owners were called Lisa and Marie Sonko, they were born in the Kingdom of Jolof as domesticated slave girls who were sold to French slave traders centuries ago. The Voodoo Gods and spirits showed them the way to liberation, and ever since then, they've been High Priestesses with unbelievable magic power. I felt forever thankful to my owners for setting me free from mortal trappings, so I could be forever young and carefree.

Over the hundreds of outfits, I also began to notice an interesting curiosity through my display window. For some reason, cars seemed to be changing shape as boxy sedans and station wagons gradually turned into more streamlined coupes and minivans. Even the store's music went from low tempoed piano music and soft jazz to this soft R&B beat and cheap covers of pop songs.

I had lived through virtually the entirety of the 1980s as a doll, and I couldn't even imagine myself as anything else than Marie and Lisa's display doll. It was my destiny to serve them by making their product look good, and l felt I would continue to serve my owners until the end of time.

Things carried on like this until it happened. A sedan with white paint and roof mounted lights pulled up in front of the store and three men walk out. Two of them were police officers while the other was a Forensic Mage with a staff topped by a cross in his right hand. They each walked in, and their steps wandered behind me until they went up to the counter and ask something that I couldn't hear over the shopping music.

My mind was racing with all the things that they could be doing to my owner. I heard a loud spell and some yelling from behind the wall. Once the yelling subsided, there was nothing but shopping music as steps become louder before walking out the front door to reveal that my owners were being taken away in these weird glowing handcuffs.

They put up a struggle, but the Mage's binding spell sucked in all of their attempted red magic. Once my owners got escorted into the back of the car, the officers stepped into the front of the police car and drove off. They kidnapped My owners and I was just mentally begging for them to save my owners.

As if that wasn't enough, a golden aura surrounded me like a giant snake before everything went black. Great, darkness—and it wasn't even night yet! My beloved window completely disappeared while ugly pillow-like walls and ceilings took their place. I fell over, for I was off the stand, and my vision was nothing but these black and brown fields. I pannicked, since I couldn't be beautiful if there was no one to be beautiful for. But I figured that I might, at least, get a new owner out of this.

But nothing else happened, since I was laying in what I could only presume to be a new kind of shipping container. I lie there for what felt like days while loud colors clouded my vision and coalesced into a vision similar to the window of my owner's shop. I wondered if I was going to be someone else's doll or up on display again or even if I'd ever be useful again!

My hopes were dashed as I heard a door open and a series of footsteps migrating their way around me before stopping. Next, I heard the following being chanted by an unseen man.

"By the power of God Almighty, I command you to return to Human form!"

Wait, Human! I mentally yelled as an unseen force overcame me, and for the first time in nearly twelve years, I felt something. Except this wasn't an emotional feeling, but one that I felt outside and like, around myself.

I felt myself becoming heavier and heavier as other strange sensations overwhelmed me. First, it was like a sensation of unbearable heat as if my entire body was tied to a space heater.

Next I sensed all sorts of disgusting fluids forming in my gut and coursing inside my pristine arms and legs. On top of that, there was all this fluid and solid weight that formed inside me that made me want to gag.

It felt more unnatural than turning plastic; Best I could describe it, it was like a fall from grace and a transition to something unclean. All the sensations combined, overwhelmed every second I was coming to life. It was so bad that the sensation of my entire body twitching played second fiddle, and I didn't even notice or even comprehend anything that happened at that point. It all became a blur until the sensations evolved and became, like, harsh pounding in my chest and electric shocks that went through what I felt was a disguising, lowly Human body.

"EWW!" I yelled. "I'M HORRENDOUS!" Now, what was hardest to get used to and I worked on this for weeks was that there was apparently thinking in my head as well as thinking by vibrating the inside of my neck. "WHERE'S MY OWNER? I NEED MY OWNER!" I screamed as the sensation of being alive was just too much for a doll to handle. "I DON'T WANT TO BE DISGUSTING. I NEED TO BE BEAUTIFUL!"

"Child," said the voice, "You are beautiful, but this is only the start of a rehab." I now felt pains in my midsection from screaming as the voice continued: "Your owners kidnapped you and got away with mass murder for hundreds of years; they will be awaiting trial."

"Trial!" I said in surprise. "No, no-no-no, you can't arrest my owners. I need to be owned. I need to be beautiful. I need to serve a purpose!"

"You're Human now," said the voice. "You need to make your own purpose."

Those words have stuck with me since that fateful March day in 1992. I spent a little over a year in that mental institution over in Franklin. My guide was a Methodist minister who helped me transition back into humanity after all those years. He did a wide array of things, ranging from teaching me how to walk to showing me how to use a computer for the first time in my life.

I was also able to see my family again, as my mother, father and older brother came all the way from Florida to visit me. It was also there that I learned about where my limbs came from. While I knew the whole time my head was all mine, but my other parts, though came from the plasticized bodies of complete strangers.

Like my hands, for instance, came from a 15-year-old girl from Dallas who disappeared on July 17th, 1979. My arms, torso, and legs came from a 25-year-old dance instructor from Missouri who had disappeared on January 16th 1977. My feet came from a 21-year-old retail clerk from Kentucky who disappeared on September 11th 1977. I'm now like an abomination of dead people's body parts, like a sexier version of Frankenstein.

As disturbing as the whole thing was, I got discharged in summer of 1993 without further complications. Since then, I've made it a point to live my life a little bit differently, and instead of going back to the career path of psychology, I decided to live my new life as if this was a reincarnation. I took out a few loans from my insurance company and I used it to open my own yoga studio.

I appreciate movement and well being now that I know what it's like for life to be taken away from me. I've been married for the past 22 years to a loving husband and even though I had to explain to my twin boys when they were kids, why they're blonde and not brown haired like me and my husband. They're both 20 years old now and I still love them as if they came out of my own flesh and blood.

One positive is that because my venture was so successful, I was able to make great use of the body parts of total strangers. This gives me an existential trip sometimes because there's times where I wonder if I still am that psychology student or did the dancer and retail clerk in me force me into owning a business like a yoga studio. I honestly don't know if I'm me, them or us, but what I do know is that I'm 61 years old, but I retain the appearance of a well-toned 30-something. Of course, some of my youth comes from a potion shop down the street from my old studio. But other than a few hiccups, Post doll life turned out well for me, and one thing's for certain: I try to not be cursed.

The End

5
THE LEGEND OF THE WERECOUGAR

It was Halloween night, 1999; the sky was dark and the full moon dominated the San Jose skyline. There was also a couple driving in a blue 1982 Ford Escort coupe on a relatively sparse highway. The car's driver was a young woman in tight-fitting blue jeans with a low-cut V-neck. The passenger, meanwhile, was dressed in a long sleeve red shirt, a pair of denim overalls, and a matching red baseball cap with the letter 'M' crudely inscribed in marker.

"Thanks for taking me to the party, Jennie," said the man.

"I'm not just taking you there," replied Jennie. "I'm going."

The man was bemused.

"But, you don't have a costume."

"Don't worry, Joel, I have it all in the glovebox," said Jennie as Joel turned on the dome light and opened the glovebox to find a plastic barrette topped with two roundish pale yellow cat ears.

"Is this all that you have?" he asked

"I have your sharpie in my pocket, I can just draw some whiskers when we get there," she answered.

"Not really much of a costume," Joel retorted before turning the dome light off.

"Oh, shut up," said Jennie turning towards an off ramp. "It's not like I have time to create a costume in between school and work!"

"You see," said Joel. "It's shit like that why I dropped out."

"I thought it was because you didn't know what you wanted out of life," Jennie chuckled.

"Well, that too," replied Joel as they drove into a parking garage. Jennie eventually found a spot on the third level where her car wouldn't be car wouldn't be sandwiched by others. She turned it off as the cassette player abruptly stopped playing music, and all was silent.

Joel opened the door as Jennie requested.

"Hey Joel, would you mind putting my parking pass in the window?"

"Oh, of course," said Joel, who rummaged through the glove box to find the Fall '99 parking permit before placing it in the window.

"You can go ahead without me. I'll be down there in a few minutes," stated Jennie.

"Oh," replied Joel walking out of the car. "I love you," he said.

"You too." She smiled as he shut the car door with a metallic clink. He reopened the door and took the seatbelt out of the doorway and into the car before he closed it again with a firm, reassuring thud.

Once Joel was long out of view and walking down the concrete steps of the parking lot, Jennie turned on her dome light, brought down her sun visor and flipped open the vanity mirror. She had taken her keys out of the ignition and put them in her right pocket. Then from the left pocket, she got out a sharpie and drew six wavy lines, three on each side of her face between her mouth and nose. She drew three curving shapes between her nose and upper lip, which gave the crude appearance of a crude cleft lip and some whiskers.

Should I color my nose? she wondered looking down at the sharpie. *Nah, I don't have another marker, it's good enough for three bucks, I suppose,* she mumbled to herself while flipping the visor back into its normal position.

She got out of the car and stepped down the concrete steps of the parking garage out onto the sidewalk. The night was bright, and cars sped past the street lamps like specters in the night. She walked down a couple of blocks as low-pitched sounds became slightly higher, and higher sounds became lower. The world started spinning as she subtly lost her balance.

Maybe I'm coming down with something… thought Jennie as her hearing slowly improved. *But I can always rest it off tonight.*

She would faintly hear techno music and the voice of a fraternity brother who stood outside of the frat house.

"Students only!" he said

"Yes, but I'm with a friend who is a UCSJ student," rebutted Joel.

"Look, until I see student ID, I'm not letting you in, Beta Phi Delta orders!" stated the frat boy as Joel sighed and walked down the sidewalk where he'd lay eyes on Jennie.

"What are you doing out here?" she asked.

"They won't let me in!" complained Joel.

"I'll go deal with him," said Jennie as Joel walked behind her. Unbeknownst to Jennie, the ears had disappeared from her barrette almost instantaneously, making it look as though she was only wearing a regular yellow barrette. "So, you won't let my boyfriend in?" she inquired.

"Listen, lady, he doesn't have a student ID handy. It's for students only!"

Jennie soon showed her student ID as her whole fingernails began to whiten as if they had been bleached.

"I'm bringing him as a guest, unless you have a problem with that," she said as her eyes slowly started turning yellow

"O-of course. By all means…" stammered the frat boy, noticing the changes. He stepped to one side and let the two in as if they were VIPs. The moment they walked in, they would be greeted to the strong scent of alcohol, cigarettes, and the blaring sound of music was practically loud enough to make the walls shake. Jennie walked past the living room, where people were dancing, and into the dining room where a buffet had been laid out, and there was everything from salad to pizza to doughnuts.

Jennie had been putting slices of pepperoni and sausage pizza on her plate while Joel, who had already eaten, was busy dancing in the living room. People were dressed up in all sorts of costumes, which ranged from plastic masks to full outfits. Jennie went to the back of the house where there was a large patio with many chairs.

"Hey Jennie!" called someone who waved to her.

"Tina!" said Jennie, walking over to a table near a small staircase that went down to a modest back lawn.

"Great costume!" complemented Tina.

"Thanks, I guess," replied Jennie, sitting down at the table, "but what are you supposed to be?" asked Jennie, eating pizza.

"You don't recognize me?" exclaimed Tina.

"No," said Jennie frankly.

"I'm Buffy the Vampire Slayer," replied Tina.

"Oh," said Jennie. "I'm not really into soaps."

"Well, I don't exactly have the talents to enchant my costumes either," said Tina, pointing at Jennie's now pink nose.

"Enchanted?" Jennie asked in a bewildered fashion.

"Because last I checked, you weren't a Felid."

Jennie soon looked down at her greasy fingers to find that her nails were consuming the ends of her digits, and there were black calluses forming beneath her fingers as well as on her palms. All she could do was stare as her hands gained a subtle fuzziness that you wouldn't see from a distance.

"Got your own tongue?" Said Tina playfully as Jennie frantically grabbed at her barrette would be only to run her claws through shortening hair.

"I-I only got it at the Salvation Army," said Jennie, panicking. "It was a barrette! How the hell was I supposed to know it was magic?"

"And I would've thought you'd stick to that vegetarian diet that you've been trying out," said Tina.

"I was," said Jennie, downing her second slice of pizza. "Do you know where the bathroom is, perchance?"

"There's one by the rec room, but there was a bit of a line last time I was there," said Tina.

"Thanks," replied Jennie, darting back into the house where the music somehow seemed a little louder than it was when she first walked in. There was only one other person waiting outside the bathroom, and he was dressed in a cowboy outfit.

"Is someone in there?" asked Jennie.

"I'm waiting for my brother," said the man.

"Well, get out of my fucking way!" she exclaimed, bearing her still Human teeth.

"Will do, miss," said the frat boy fearfully as he'd proceed to step over a small barrier upstairs to use the toilet up there.

The door opened, revealing another fraternity brother riding on an inflatable horse with only the top half in a checkered button up shirt as he'd walk out with a wide gaze.

"Kyle?" he asked, looking around as Jennie quickly ran in to find that pale yellow fur had taken over her head as white fur appeared beneath her now actually splitting lip. She was speechless as she opened her eyes wide, and she watched her now rounded-triangle shaped ears move to the top of her head. Her chest had already been flattening as her V-neck sagged against growing fur.

Yet despite these changes, only her feet felt sore and compressed. She untied her sneakers and took her socks off to find that her feet had gained claws, fur, and their arches were becoming more of an ankle. This gave her natural high heels as canines slowly grew into fangs before she proceeded to walk out of the bathroom as all who were in the rec room were drunk and nauseous.

Jennie growled subtly as drunken prey was fine for hunting. She walked towards them as a white flash came from one of the guest's cameras that was soon accompanied by a clicking and a mechanical whirring noise. She then ran to the couches that surrounded the TV and simply let basic urges take over. She pounced on the couch and clawed at a man's chest, biting his arm. The rest screamed bloody murder before their entrails were laid around the couch and the guy that took the picture ran away with her camera. Jennie soon developed more of a maw, which let the completely furred huntress gut her prey. The lady with the camera had gone into the living room and frantically turned off the CD changer.

"There's a Werecougar here!" she exclaimed. "Somebody call animal control!"

"Turn the damn music back on!" complained a drunken guest.

"Not until we get out of here—unless you want to be dinner!"

Joel's face lost all color as he imagined that Jennie was one of its victims. Tina heard the commotion and nervously walked inside, where Jennie had eviscerated most of the guests and even sported a fully grown tail through ripped up jeans.

"My home…my mate," groaned Jennie, jabbing her claws into Tina. She eviscerated her as she'd leave great chunks of flesh, bone, and muscle exposed to the elements. It was then that Joel looked into the dining room to find freshly killed bodies on a shag carpet lined with intestines and paw print shaped bloodstains.

"Me want you," groaned Jennie as the lady with the camera took another picture of her. "Me want kittens."

Joel soon ran along with everyone else save for a guest dressed as Dracula, who ran to the cordless phone to call the police. Jennie bit into Joel's shoulder and sucked on it as if he were made of hard candy. After the last guest hung up, he frantically ran out the door as cries of pain emanated from the otherwise quiet living room.

Joel's hair quickly receded into his skull as his shoes and the bottoms of his overalls were quickly ripped up. His eyes turned green and circular as cries of pain turned to roaring. Claws emanated from his fingers as his face distorted, pressing his ever-pinking nose outward and his pointing ears were shoved to the top of his head. Fur and a tail had long sprouted, and once his changes stopped, he was nearly an exact replica of Jennie save for being male.

Jennie let go of her mate before walking back into the rec room, where she would soon lay down and claw all the clothes off her body, as she didn't need more hides than what she already had. Joel laid down on the living room couch and did the same thing, groaning as he clawed through his overalls and shirt like butter until he lay naked

They licked themselves before going to sleep. They awoke with a start as odd roaring and strangely colored sunlight permeated through the front window. Jennie's ears perked as she got up off the couch and bore her teeth, since no one had the right to be in her domain. She dragged her hind paws across the carpet to show those other cats who was boss. Joel, meanwhile, had curled up in fear, as he didn't know what to make of anything.

Black hided humans walked in with large, black sticks. Jennie growled to keep the invaders away before bearing her razor sharp fangs. One moment, there was a sharp jab on her top right nipple; the next all was black. Joel bore his teeth at the humans to avenge his mate, but he, too, felt a sharp pain in his arm, and like Jennie, all was black thereafter.

That was the last anyone had seen or heard from Joel Dunton and Jennie Smith. Only one clear photo remains of the beast. The witch who enchanted the barrette in the first place remains at large to this very day, as there wasn't any paperwork about such a donation. The costume had long been fused with Jennie, and both of them have to spend the rest of their lives at Big Basin in the Santa Cruz mountain range.

It is unknown how large their litters are in comparison to other werecougar specimens found in the Rockies or the Pacific Northwest, but some say they have the intelligence of humans and kidnap their prey before consuming them. Sometimes, they are kidnapped without a trace, and local legends say that the presence of a once extinct species is the cause of nearly all missing persons in San Lorenzo Valley.

Will you be next?

The End

6
TRICK WISH GRANTING

One summer day in the Asian side of Istanbul, there was a small antique shop that had a modest looking overhang which read "Çimen Antika est. 1935" Like many antique shops, Jewelry and other ornaments glistened in the the front window. Just inside was a young woman of 19 years named Zehra. She was a petite Human woman with short black hair, a soft narrow face, almond brown skin and looming fears of the future as she dusted off an Ottoman quran near the back of the shop, making herself useful for nobody.

Droning silence persisted for hours as people walked past as if the shop didn't exist. The fact that it was on a crowded street in the city didn't help matters either as everyone bypassed the store in favor of other shops, restaurants, and coffee houses. Few walked in at any given time of day, and those who did, just came in to look at the merchandise and walk out as if the store was a free museum.

This went on for hours until a man of 57 walked in with a large oil lamp. The lamp was made of silver and featured a large bulb shape with Ottoman calligraphy atop its round base. It was also tall and towered into a central hollow spire, providing space for an oil flame to appear while a shiny, black tarnish had coated the lamp, and its intricate patterns as a result of decades of decay.

"How can I help you?" asked Zehra, seeing the man walk in.

"I would like to sell my antique lamp," said the man.

Zehra then took the silver artifact and put it on the counter.

"Where did you get this?" she inquired.

"I inherited it from my grandfather," the man answered.

"Grandfather?" she inquired, noticing the man's head of gray hair.

"He lived to be 109," the man explained. "Now that he's dead, I figured that I may as well get his things off my hands."

"So, how much do you want to sell it?" asked Zehra casually

The man thought for a moment before saying, "Three thousand lire."

Zehra was shocked.

"Wait, three THOUSAND lire?"

"Yes," said the man confidently

"From the looks of it, I'd be more willing to go to 300," she said frankly.

"Ah," mused the man. "But this isn't just any lamp. It contains a Genie."

"Genie?" said Zehra, hiding her excitement

"Yes," said the man. "He's the reason why I'm even standing here right now!"

She thought for a moment, looking down at the lamp while analyzing its every crevice.

"Three thousand it is," she said, bringing her hand out before the man shook it. Next, Zehra emptied the cash register of bills ranging from fives to two-hundreds until the man had a handful of assorted banknotes. "Have a good day," said Zehra, giving the man his money.

"You too," he replied as he proceeded to walk out the door.

Once the man was out of sight, she looked down at the lamp, pondering all the things she could wish for.

Hope this works, thought Zehra nervously as she gingerly meandered her hand down toward the lower end of its bulb before gently rubbing it. Heat began radiating inside the lamp like a laptop powering up as the black tarnish dispelled itself while sandy yellow smoke billowed out of the lamp's open wick. The smoke became denser while billowing downwards toward the floor opposite of Zehra.

The smoke stopped emanating out of the lamp, for it was already forming into an imposing, dark-yellow figure. The figure filled itself out as a Genie of stocky build with a long black beard & rough, calloused, yellow skin. The man stared at Zehra briefly before saying, "Ah, you must be my new master."

"I guess I am," replied Zehra with a smile as the Genie stared at her.

"Well, I'm proud to serve you" he said, looking around at the antiques. "But first, would you mind if I ask you a question?"

"Of course," said Zehra confidently

"Well, what year it?" asked the Genie

"Twenty-fifteen," answered Zehra. "Why? When was the last time you were out or whatever?"

"Last time I was summoned, radio was a luxury," answered the Genie with a laugh.

"So, I assume you grant wishes right?" asked Zehra awkwardly.

"Yes, but I'd rather not talk about it out here," stated the Genie looking towards the window. "Is there somewhere private we can talk?"

"We can talk in the office," said Zehra.

"Of course," replied the Genie "Lead the way, Master."

Zehra walked out from behind the register toward the jewelry cabinet, where a wooden door with the words "Employees Only" on a small black sign. She opened the door, and inside lay a computer set on top of a wooden desk, an array of filing cabinets, and a small, steel safe. Zehra sat down in the chair by the computer before turning around to face the genie.

"As you might be aware," said the nude Genie standing in front of the safe, "I can grant up to three wishes, and they can be anything you want; money, power, or anything else your heart desires."

"Oh really?" said Zehra, grinning at the possibilities. "Well then, I wish that this store never went out of business."

"Of course," said the Genie as Zehra grabbed a post-it off the computer's square-shaped monitor. The note had the safe combination written on it. The genie, meanwhile, conjured silver-colored energy in his right hand while turning toward the safe. Zehra turned around in her chair to see the magnificent power of her newfound slave for the energy grew denser until it resembled a glowing fluid ball. Once the ball was at its full capacity, the genie fired it at the safe as a long, unwavering beam of light.

Once the energy beam stopped, Zehra got up out of her chair, and with the combination in hand, she twirled the safe's lock—78-12-23—before pulling down the latch and opening its door.

In an alcove above storage compartments containing the deed to the store and a total of 250,000 lire in life savings, there was a large stack of pure silver coins. Zehra looked at the safe, mystified at the addition of the coins, so she scooped out an armful only to have them all pile up on the floor. The next time Zehra looked up, another stack of coins had appeared from nowhere.

"I've enchanted the safe to provide an endless amount of pure silver," said the genie as Zehra continued hoarding a great pile of coins. She grabbed one coin and inspected it. The coin had uneven circular ridges surrounding an inscription in Ottoman Turkish calligraphy. Zehra would comment, but she was too elated to care.

"Thank you—uuhh…?" she paused, not knowing what to call him.

"Hakan," said the Genie humbly. "You can just call me Hakan."

"You have no idea how much this means to us!" Zehra exclaimed, hugging Hakan.

"I'm always happy to be of service," he said, patting the top of her head.

"Now, it might be a while before my next wish, but would you like to help me out in the meantime?" asked Zehra

"I would be honored," said Hakan. "It's just so dark and lonely in there."

"Great, you can work the cash register because you seem to know your money," stated Zehra, walking back out to the store front.

"Oh I have experience with money" He stated before his smile would become a befuddled frown when there was a bizzare plastic contraption with a screen, two large metal boxes, several wires and a few lights. Zehra would show him everything from how to use the mouse to what button to press in order to open the register. She even taught him how to manage inventory and debt spreadsheets on the shop's shared drive.

A few hours later, Zehra and Hakan stood behind the register as every item had been cleaned and well dusted. Suddenly, the back door opened, and in came Yilmaz, a balding middle-aged man of 48 dressed in a button-down shirt & jeans. He was carrying an armful of vintage LPs he had gotten at an estate sale. He wandered down the hall towards a rack containing other albums and singles. He filed the records in before he walked up the aisle toward the register.

"Hey sweetie," greeted Yilmaz.

"Dad," said Zehra. "How was the sale?"

"It was alright," replied Yilmaz. "I mean, I got some small stuff, but nothing too valuable." Yilmaz' expression turned to anger once he lay eyes on the Genie and his apparent lamp.

"Well, that's good, I guess," she replied.

"Zehra!" he said. "How would you like to explain HIM!" He pointed at Hakan.

"Well, he came from this antique lamp that I paid 3,000 lire for!" Zehra said, pointing at the silver lamp.

"With all due respect," said Hakan, "this lady is my master."

"You people are nothing but trouble!" exclaimed Yilmaz, pointing at Hakan.

"Dad," said Zehra with an unbelieving grin. "He's a kind Genie who helped us with our debt."

"Zehra," replied Yilmaz. "Genies are servants of Iblis."

"But Dad," said Zehra meekly. "They're not all like that. Hakan here is actually very nice."

Yilmaz sighed, saying, "Listen, he may well have helped out our debt, but I'm sorry to say that they're all the same. They grant your wishes, but then at what cost? He probably put monopoly money in the safe or something! I was watching the news recently, and they were talkin' about someone who wished for a simpler life and wound up homeless while the genie stole the poor guy's home!"

Hakan replied with a sly grin, "I don't know what Monopoly money is, but I placed silver coins in the safe that you can still cash in!"

"I DON'T WANT TO HEAR FROM YOU!" exclaimed Yilmaz.

"So what!" argued Zehra. "One Genie does something bad, and they're all evil?"

"No," replied Yilmaz. "That's not what I'm saying. What I'm saying is that you can't trust a genie to make your dreams come true, even if it's something you pray for. Besides, I don't want a bunch of Demons running around my shop!"

"Dad!" exclaimed Zehra.

"I don't want to hear it, Zehra," scolded Yilmaz. "You're an embarrassment to the Çimen family and your great grandfather's legacy since you've forsaken this establishment!"

"That's it!" she said, turning toward Hakan. "Hakan, I wish my father wasn't so stubborn!"

"Oh, don't you dare make wishes in my—" Yilmaz was interrupted by an invisible force that wiped his subconscious clean. His face went from intense rage to contented bliss in a matter of seconds.

"There," said Hakan, "that'll put a stop to that."

"Dad?" said Zehra. "Are you okay with Hakan now?"

"Of course, sweetie," said Yilmaz with glossed over eyes. "I'm fine with whatever."

"Even driving right back home," replied Zehra with a satisfied smile while pointing toward the back door.

"Indeed," he said. "In fact, I trust you with the store so much that I'll leave early." He proceeded to walk out the back door right down the alleyway to his car.

Later, the shop neared closing time, and Hakan was working the register, just as he'd been trained to do by her. Zehra, meanwhile, walked up to the front window and twisted the sign around from "Open" to "closed." She sighed as she walked back to the register where Hakan had already turned it off.

"Is there anything wrong, Master?" asked Hakan.

"Just follow me, and I'll tell you," replied Zehra, walking out the front door. Hakan grabbed his lamp and walked out the front door before Zehra locked the store. As the two walked down the street, people looked at them and reacted with everything from awestruck envy to deep seeded contempt.

"I think I shouldn't have made that wish," sighed Zehra regretfully as she started down the street.

"What do you mean?" asked Hakan, walking behind her while analyzing the clothing people wear in the present.

"The wish that made Dad less stubborn," replied Zehra. "What if I made him lose his personality?"

"Now, there, there…" said Hakan, wrapping his coarse arm around her. "He'll still love you. All I did was make his mind more flexible, as it were."

Zehra sighed.

"Yes, but was it right? What if my father stops caring about the shop!"

"He won't need to," said Hakan, following his master into a nearby parking garage. "That safe now has infinite coins. He won't have to worry about money ever again."

Zehra walked down the concrete stairs.

"Well, can I at least reverse the wish?" she asked.

"I'm quite sorry, Master," replied Hakan. "But I can only grant wishes, not reverse them. I'm not God, y'know."

Zehra was mystified by Hakan's words.

"Wait," she said, walking through the basement level parking lot. "I thought you Genies had unlimited power!"

"Well, what if I told you that I wasn't always a Genie?" said Hakan.

"Really?" inquired Zehra, unlocking her silver 2004 Renault Clio, a rotund hatchback with only two doors, a slightly scraped up front bumper, and a humble hood. Hakan stood on the righthand side of the car, completely clueless of how to get in.

"Lift the handle and open up," she explained, sitting down into the driver's seat and unlocking the passenger side door.

Hakan did just that before sitting down on the passenger seat and placing his lamp on the floor. He gazed across the car's dash, mystified by its vents, dials, and electronics. When Zehra turned the key, Hakan's ears were bombarded with strange, deep bass sounds and odd-sounding drums that seemed to go with the bass.

"What's that noise?" he complained

"It's just the radio," said Zehra, turning the music off. "All cars have radios now."

"Yes, but must they have such weird and loud music!" complained Hakan.

"That's what music sounds like now," said Zehra

"And what are these dreaded tones?" complained Hakan

"It's the car telling you to put your seat belt on, they can go way faster now" explained Zehra "It should be on your right, just put the metal part into the little slit next to the red button."

After some trial and error, Hakan buckled up and Zehra backed out of the parking space. "But anyway, you were saying?"

Once the car got going, he told her the following...

Well, way back in the seventeenth century, I was Human, just like you. My folks were well to do Kurdish merchants, and I worked as a secretary for a Naga banker by the name of Jorin Bersinji. I spent my days transcribing letters and sorting through the guy's mail. He was nice, personable, and an all-around great guy to work for.

In those days, we didn't have lire bills, lire coins, or even one of those bimetallic kuruş coins. Our currency was made of only two coins: the silver akçe and the golden para. There were three akçe in a para, and I would tally up which accounts had what coins for their bank statements, so I was always kept busy. In 1688, the Viziers introduced a new type of coin that was their answer to the inflation problem at the time.

It was this large, silver coin called the kuruş, which in those days was somehow worth 40 para or 120 akçe. This made everyone's job difficult, as transactions were harder, and we had to completely rethink the way we sorted the coins.

More and more kuruş came into our bank, and we gained

debts since all of our assets in silver were now virtually worthless. I was drowning in long division, debt, and now liquid assets. Our scales for weighing coins were useless, and there were lines out the door. It was a hectic time for us until Jorin had us melt all the akçe into more valuable kuruş, so we could pay off our debts and surcharges.

When there weren't enough akçe to melt, he had me and other bank employees steal money out of innocent people's bank accounts and carry these sacks of coins in an armored coach. I will never forget holding that musket in my arms on our way to the foothills. It was barely a few days before Ramadan when we got to those foothills in the middle of nowhere away from farms, roads, and trails.

Much to my shock, he had bribed a group of Imams and builders to make his mint. When I asked him about it, he said that this scheme would make me rich, when in reality I grew to become his henchman for his newfound enterprise. I probably made millions of those counterfeit coins, and we'd use the coins to buy anything—slaves, jewelry, turbans, mansions, guns, unicorns, you name it!

Best part was all the merchants in those days were illiterate so they couldn't tell if the calligraphy was off or if letters missing or even if words were misspelled so we didn't even have to be all that precise with our minting, it just needed to look real enough and we could fool them! This went on for ten years, and by that time, we had sold the bank and became bandits at war with Seymens and other groups of bandits.

I have personally shot, mugged, and raped innocent people. It felt good and natural after a while, but eventually, knights on horseback came to our mint in full force and killed most of us by sword, leaving only me, Jorin, and two others.

They arrested and tried us in Sharia Court for embezzlement, fraud, murder, and worst yet, treason. They had us all sentenced to death. I was impaled on a hook along with Jorin for the gawking public to witness. God knows what happened to the other guys, but I can't imagine it was any worse than what I went through. For obvious reasons, I went down to hell to be punished eternally for my egregious sins. And boy was I punished.

I was sold into the Cini slave trade and made into a target dummy for them to practice shooting muskets. I couldn't move or speak, for all I could do was get pelted with round after round of lead balls. When there was peacetime, they turned me Human and grilled me over open bonfire before they all ate me. I was digested and pooped, then they reformed me again into uman soup, and used fire magic to heat me up before they fed me to the neighborhood bums.

I went back to being used as a practice dummy again once war started again. I would be in a row of other dummies where I'd get hundreds of rounds worth of enchanted musket balls. Once the army had trained, they left me there with a stomach full of lead. Finally, an elderly Demon with blue, wrinkled skin and long, yellowish white tusks turned me Human again while he held up this silver oil lamp.

"I know of a way to end your suffering," he said. "I can turn you into a Genie and you'll live in this lamp; or you can continue your torment."

After forty years of constant abuse, I accepted the deal in a heartbeat. He gave me a lamp to live in and made me into this rough, yellow form that you see now. He also endowed me with incredible magical abilities, so I could best use magic to serve my master, and the rest is history.

>─┼─◄►─•─Ο─•─◄►─┼─◄

Zehra had been driving while listening to Hakan's life story. She teared up as she drove on the freeway while navigating traffic. Hakan ended his story as Zehra drove away from the impending bumper-to-bumper traffic down to an off ramp leading to a neighborhood chocked with fairly tall apartment buildings.

"No wonder you guys are so tricky," said Zehra, stopping at a red traffic light. "Hundreds of years of total darkness would make me tricky, too!"

"You don't know the half of it!" said Hakan as the light went green, causing Zehra to drive down the street. She drove past a few more lights before getting to a different neighborhood of ever shrinking appartment complexes. Zehra didn't want to hear any more about the life, or lack thereof, of Genies. She drove down the road to find her father's car parked in the driveway with the engine still idling.

Zehra's 45-year-old mother, Melek, and 78-year-old grandmother, Fatma, stood outside of the car, looking concerned for Yilmaz as he sat behind the wheel blankly. Zehra parked her car out by the curb and turned it off.

"Pull the plastic handle and push the door out," explained Zehra, walking out of the car and out onto the street. Hakan opened his door and grabbed his lamp before stepping out of the car, closing the door with his butt.

Zehra stepped up to her father's dark blue 2010 Corolla, where he gazed blankly at the garage.

"What's going on?" asked Zehra.

"Your father has been acting strange lately," said Fatma.

"What do you mean, Gramma?" asked Zehra.

"Your father only does what we tell him, Zehra," said Melek befuddled. "He's lost his whole personality!"

Zehra's heart sank as Hakan walked up behind the concerned group.

Fatma spotted the yellow man walking towards Zehra as her gaze turned to anger.

"Zehra," she said. "Did you do this?"

"Did I do what?" answered Zehra.

"Did you wish that curse on your father!" exclaimed Fatma.

"With all due respect, ma'am," said Hakan with a sleazy grin, "my master only wished that he was less stubborn, and wishes aren't the most reliable of things, y'know."

Fatma looked down at Hakan's lamp and asked, "How did you end up with my granddaughter?"

"I bought him at the store from this guy for 3,000 lire," explained Zehra "The store was so close to closing that I figured to buy the lamp and wish the store never went out of business."

"You did what!" exclaimed Fatma.

"If you've seen the store lately," argued Zehra, "it's so close to bankruptcy that it's not even funny, and the risk was worth the reward."

"I'll have you know that when I owned the store, we were nearing closure then, too!" exclaimed Fatma.

"Fatma," said Melek. "He may well be a Demon, but this is our last hope."

"That's what Mehmed said during the clash!" exclaimed Fatma, pointing at Hakan, "but I never stooped so low as to resort to overpriced Genies to bail us out!"

While they argued, Zehra motioned Hakan to follow her down the street.

"You better not be making any more wishes!" exclaimed Fatma.

"Fatma, stop it!" argued Melek. "Zehra was only trying to help!"

Zehra and Hakan walked down the street, so she could make her last wish in relative privacy.

"Hakan," she said, "I really wish I had more control over these wishes!"

Hakan concentrated smokey brown-colored energy in his palms before releasing them onto his master. The smoke billowed until it surrounded Zehra, completely consuming her very being. Next, the smoke funnelled itself into the lamp like dust attracted to a vacuum cleaner. Once the smoke dissipated into the lamp, it revealed nothing but thin air.

Hakan, not having a master, anymore started glowing a whitish tan color as life returned to his body for the first time in nearly 320 years. His genitals returned, along with his internal organs, and rough, yellow flesh became light tan skin. He immediately doubled over in pain once centuries old scars formed on his back and stomach. The scars were dark red scabs surrounded by bruising at the exact places the hook impaled them hundreds of years earlier. Hakan was Human again, shivering against the relatively cool 15 degree air, butt naked in public.

I wonder if I still have my powers… thought Hakan, setting down Zehra's lamp before conjuring white energy in his palm. *Hey, this works after all,* he thought before hurling it at himself like a bag of loose powder. The energy would recombine into a button-down shirt, a pair of slacks with a leather belt, a pair of leather heeled shoes, and a white, generic baseball cap. Once Hakan was dressed, he grabbed the lamp and walked over to the Çimen family.

Yilmaz' car had turned off, and he was standing in front of his house.

"Don't worry, I feel wonderful now," said Yilmaz. "It's like I'm more content now, thanks to that Genie"

"I still don't think Zehra should've bought him!" pouted Fatma.

"Let's just drop this," said Melek. "All this is doing is accomplishing nothing!"

Once Hakan stood before them, he set down the lamp and casted a spell of white fluid energy that flew into each of their ears.

"Genies are always bad news!" exclaimed Fatma. "They were tricky con artists in my day, and they—" she was interrupted by the spell as it made both their thoughts and words go silent.

"What were we talking about?" asked Fatma.

"I'm sorry to say this," said Hakan, "but it seems your daughter died in a car crash."

Their faces turned to sadness, for any memory of Zehra coming home was deleted from their mind.

"She was so young…" sniffled Yilmaz.

"There, there," said Hakan, patting Yilmaz's back. "Let's go inside, so we can talk about it."

Everyone walked into the house, but Zehra's car remained parked at the curb, vacant.

A couple months passed, and a random corpse was grounded into a paste and buried. The shop could not be salvaged. The windows were all boarded up, and the sign was taken down. The centuries old sorcerer, Hakan, teleported into the boarded-up building where all the merchandise still sat unsold. He walked over toward Yilmaz's old safe before twisting the lock around in the combination.

He opened the safe and grabbed a large handful of silver coins before summoning multicolored energy. The energy swirled around the coins, causing them to flatten and become multicolored slips of paper. The paper manifested once the spell wore off, and he now had 30,000 lire worth of notes. He placed the notes into a leather wallet before vanishing into thin air. The lamp, however, sat alone where the computer once was. Zehra awaited a master, but her lamp remained in the great vault that was a small antique store on the Asian side of Istanbul.

The End

7
IDENTITY AND BEING

It was a cool December night in a video game store in an Albuqurque strip mall. The sky was clear and black while cars came and went. Subtle traffic noise broke through the store's background music while nearby roads were crowded with swiftly moving traffic. People walked up and down the shelves of new and used video games as if they were books in a library. The cashier stood behind the register in his normal red uniform, waiting for someone to make a purchase.

All was normal until a man walked in with a used Xbox One game in his right hand. The cashier stared at him before directing his gaze back to the register's monitor, for the man was an unusual sight to behold. The man had a tall, muscular physique and wore tight fitting yoga pants and a light blue jacket. His peach-colored face was clean shaven and full of eyeliner, foundation, and crimson-red lipstick. Straight dirty blonde hair framed both sides of his face as he got up to the front counter, fidgeting with each step while towering over the cashier.

"How can I help you, sir?" asked the cashier.

"I beg your pardon," he said, putting the game on the counter. "I would just like to return this game."

"Well, sir, can I see the receipt?" asked the cashier.

"It's ma'am to you" she said, presenting the receipt.

The cashier hid a smirk, saying, "Alright, can I see your receipt, si—er, ma'am."

"Here you go!" said the woman, tossing her credit card and receipt on the counter.

"Dude, what's your problem?" asked a customer who had just stopped browsing through the clearance bin.

"I don't identify as a dude," corrected the woman. "I'm a transwoman, and I'm offended."

"Sorry you feel that way…" said the cashier reading her credit card, "Stephanie."

"Sorry doesn't cover half of it!" retorted Stephanie while the other customer got out his phone and promptly started recording.

"You guys—"

"EXCUSE ME, IT'S MA'AM!" Stephanie turned to the customer and said, "IT'S MA'AM."

The cashier shook with fear as he said, "I-I did say ma'am…"

"No, you said sir," argued Stephanie.

"I said you guys," said the cashier. "It's plural."

"No! Earlier you said sir," said Stephanie. "DON'T LIE TO ME. YOU SAID SIR!"

"Yes, but I said you guys, it's general," said the cashier.

"It's ma'am! The amount of times I've fucking been misgendered in this store is just disgusting!" exclaimed Stephanie. "And you need to apologize!"

"Right, ma'am, calm down!" said the cashier before Stephanie growled in his face and walked over to a promotional display. "Uhggg!" she said, forcefully kicking the display over, causing it to fall over onto another pre-owned games bin. It developed a few crease marks from the kick as Stephanie stormed back to the register. "What's your legal name!" she asked profusely. "I fucking need your full legal name!"

"That is none of your business, ma'am!" said the cashier frantically.

"Yes, that is my fucking business!" bickered Stephanie, grabbing the cashier by his shirt. "Give me your full legal name or else you'll hear from the LGBT community!"

The cashier quivered in fear.

"S-Stanley Lawrence Johnson," he stuttered.

Stephanie soon gave the cashier a great punch to the jaw, leaving behind a large bruise. The cashier felt faint as his mouth filled with blood before Stephanie gave the cashier yet another punch to the head. Stephanie let go of Stanley's shirt as he fell onto the counter face first before limply falling down toward the store's lefthand side, unconscious.

"This is what you fucking get for assuming my gender!" exclaimed Stephanie before storming out of the store with her game in hand as the customer stopped recording and promptly called the police.

The strip mall had a modestly large parking lot that practically served as a barrier between the stores and the street.

"I'll report that goddamn son of a bitch!" muttered Stephanie to herself while doing a hand-fisted gesture. "He will pay for his transphobic bigotry!"

He stormed through the parking lot up a concrete ramp towards a black steel bus shelter. The bus stop was empty save for a young woman who had dark bronze colored skin and long, jet-black hair as a turquoise necklace framed her plaid jacket. She was quietly playing games on her phone as Stephanie bitterly sat down right next to her.

"Dude, what's your problem?" said the woman, looking up towards her.

"E-excuse me," said Stephanie, twitching slightly.

"You just seem so angry," the woman replied.

"Well, if I wasn't misgendered so fucking much, I wouldn't be so angry!" exclaimed Stephanie as the woman made a smirk.

"Listen," she said. "I was a man a couple months ago. The medicine man at my old reservation turned me into a woman. I was once Nichaad, but now I am Nascha."

"You know my struggle then," stated Stephanie.

"The difference is that I identified as a woman, but was born into the wrong body!" explained Nascha before angrily pouting at Stephanie. "I paid them no mind, until I saved up the money for the Medicine Man to give me the body that I need. What's your excuse!"

"Well, I am gender non-conforming," said Stephanie in a sour tone. "Everyone should understand that!"

"Well, people also hear voices in their head, but I don't simply pretend that invisible people are real or anything!" exclaimed Nascha.

"I'm sorry, it is a real fucking thing!" protested Stephanie. "You of all people should know that!"

"I know that more people are transitioning these days, but I also know that you, sir, give folks like me a bad rep!" argued Nascha.

"It's ma'am!" said Stephanie. "If you don't think so, then fucking fight me, bigot!"

"I really don't want to," said Nascha, taking a deep breath. "I've got better things to do"

"Internalized oppression is no excuse. You're LGBT, too!" exclaimed Stephanie, punching the inside of her palm.

"S-s-so?" shuddered Nascha.

"I'm my own pers—"

And just like that, she was punched upside the head. Stephanie kicked her in the shin and beat her across the stomach. Nascha was overpowered and couldn't fight back as Stephanie kept pounding her until she was bruised, bleeding, and unconscious. She fell backwards toward the ground. Her clothes were bloodstained, as she had fallen backwards with a great thud followed by slight crack.

Stephanie took several deep breaths as she got a napkin out from her pants and wiped off the streak of blood from her hands. She collected herself in a weird sense of relief as a bus came up the street and stopped by the shelter. It proceeded to kneel one side to the curb.

"Route 48," announced the bus as it opened its door. "Glenwood Hills via Menaul."

Stephanie walked on and quietly inserted her bus pass into a tall console that stood by the bus driver.

"Fare deducted," said the console's synthetic sounding voice as it was followed by a beep. She walked past the hobos who sat closer to the front of the bus and proceeded to grab a grey rubber handle that dangled from a stainless steel pole. The bus drove away from the crime scene as part of the usual route while other passengers largely ignored her while a couple averted their gaze. Several blocks later, sirens could be heard from the distance while a smug smirk came over Stephanie's face.

Nascha later opened her eyes to discover a sterile hospital room with a blue curtain where nurses and a couple of detectives were looking overhead. One of them was pale and wore khakis with a button-down shirt. The other was a deep brown Human with long, black hair touching the shoulders of their pressed coat, as they had glowing white magic vaguely shaped like a magpie in their left hand that faded away.

"Wh-where am I?" asked Nascha once her vision came into focus and the droning sound of the heart monitor's beep bombarded her ears.

"You're in the hospital," replied the nurse watching her vitals

"How long was I out?" asked Nascha

"About 5 days" said the nurse as Nascha looked to find the two detectives looking down at her.

"Would you mind telling us what happened?" asked one of the detectives.

"Uhh," groaned Nascha, looking down at her large bandages "Last I remember, there was this guy who argued with me about something, and then everything went black."

"What would you say he looked like?" asked the detective.

"He was tall, large, and had blonde hair," answered Nascha.

"I see," said the detective. "Is there anything else you remember?"

"Well, I was at a bus stop, but that's it, sir," said Nascha. "I don't remember where I was."

"Well, ma'am, thank you for your time," said the detective, walking out of the room.

"You're welcome," replied Nascha as the detectives walked through the curtain toward where two Albuquerque police officers stood by, looking at the detectives.

"Well Shiladeezi, what did she say?"

"Memory is very spotty," said Shiladeezi, "but it corroborates with the clerk's story."

"You certainly don't think they're the same person," stated the officer. "Do you?"

"It's highly unlikely for two patients to be admitted with similar injuries within minutes of each other & from the same part of town," said other detective. "Not to mention how their descriptions were nearly identical. Therefore, the perpetrator might've been the same person."

Shiladeezi got out a medicine wheel and took their phone out of their pocket.

"Well, while I'm here, I might as well go through her memories and transfer them to my phone" said Shiladeezi. Before they soon got out their phone and unlocked it. They walked into Nascha's room chanting in a language she hadn't heard in months "From the northern winds, make the mind recall the damage of incidents."

The medicine wheel glowed orange before the phone opened a scrying app by itself. They developed vague images of the attacker in their mind as she had brutally beat her with trauma heavily staining the image. "What the hell?!" exclaimed Nascha being startled by a traumatic flashback.

"I'm so sorry" consoled Shiladeezi "I needed to probe your memories a little to see definitively if the same perpetrator on the surveillance video is the same as what you, as a witness remember "It's alright" she said before she asked in Navajo "Were you ever practicing in Pinedale by any chance"

"No, I was up in Window rock," replied Shiladeezi. "Why do you ask?"

"Because the Shaman over there is two-spirit as well" explained Nascha "You kind of look like them, so I was wondering if you were them."

"Well, I'm not and I'd love to stay and chat," said Shiladeezi "but I've got a case to solve"

"Bye" said Nascha weakly waving from her bed. Shiladeezi meanwhile, pressed the home button twice before scrolling to the email app. The email was from the Forensic Analysis Division with the title being 'Suspect' with blacked out pictures of a credit card and screen grabs of surveillance camera video showing Stephanie's face as attachments to the email.

"Suspect: Stephen McDowell, alias Stephanie McDowell," read the email as Shiladeezi scrolled down the list. It revealed public records, such as his workplace, income, and address. They pressed their phone's home button twice in order to go back to the scrying app where the memory from the witness was kept. "That's them!" they muttered to themself before they forwarded the report some of the other officers.

"I have an idea," said Shiladeezi "You call the judge for a warrant, and I'll go do something to set the suspect straight."

"What was your idea?" asked the officer.

"My idea is to actually turn him female as a favor to his identity."

"But why would the judge agree at this hour?" asked the other officer.

"We've got reasonable suspicion of an assault perpetrator," said Shiladeezi. "An arrest is an arrest; no one will know I was ever there. I can teleport over there."

The officer walked out into the hospital hallway and got out her phone, so she could call the Bernalillo County judge. Shiladeezi soon joined the officer in the hospital waiting room, sitting down on a bench by an elevator.

When the officer was done, she walked back into the waiting room and said, "He gave us the warrant."

"Great!" said Shiladeezi. "I'll be at the perp's house, and you'll get there just when I have left." They casted invisible magic into the four-parted wheel and vanishing into thin air. But instead of being in Stephanie's house, they were in a white sandy desert with a colorful sky and whisping spirits phasing in and out of existence.

They were all too familiar with this place for it was the spirit heaven, a place where Shamen commune with the spirits through their minds and souls. The spirits would soon coalesce into a black-and-white magpie Harpy with long tail feathers and impressive wing-arms. He sported a modest pattern of white underfeathers clashing with black scales and black top feathers.

"Matowits" said Shiladeezi "What brings your visage to me"

"Elder Shiladeezi" said Matowits trying to keep the meeting formal "Involuntarily transforming someone is nourishing the bad wolf inside."

It was then two wolves appeared, one wearing a collar and sitting in the ground like a pet dog and the other poofed outward bearing a mouth full of sharp teeth. "No!" exclaimed Shilazeezi "I didn't mean for it to come to this!"

Matowits perched himself on Shiladeezi's shoulder "This could set your ghost down a dark path leading to the lowest Hells." he said, "Which is shameful when you were gifted the power of magic by virtue of your birth."

"Don't remind me, sir" said Shiladeezi, embarrassed "I only wanted to run a winery at first, I never wanted to be a Shaman or a Mage of any kind. Stephanie is living a lie the way I have for centuries."

"That resentment is feeding the bad wolf" said Matowits as the snarling wolf grew to be giant. "It's rare for mortal Humans to naturally have both a masculine and feminine aspect in spirit and body. You may not be willing all the time, but Magic is your gift and such a marvelous gift shouldn't be wasted on vengeance."

The giant bad wolf snarled over Shiladeezi's head before they sized up what to say next "It's not vengeance, but justice" said Shiladeezi as the bad wolf began to shrink down to Shiladeezi's eye level.

"I have the warrent and the will to enact both worldly and spiritual justice on the assailant that alluded us. The media would go mad with a case like this and the quieter we can make it, the less chaos there will be in the long run."

It was then the Good wolf grew to be as tall as Shiladeezi as the good wolf could be seen attacking the bad wolf, biting and scratching it with the bad wolf being just as ferocious in return.

"I might not approve the means, but I appreciate the thought you put behind it" said Matowits before Shiladeezi found themself tired and standing in a studio apartment behind the couch where Stephanie was lying down while, typing furiously on his laptop. Shiladeezi laid down on the floor and quietly inched beneath the couch, catching their breath so their spirit energy could recharge. They lay down for a good minute before quietly chanting, "I call upon the eastern wind to spread my feminine aspect unto Stephanie, to change him from man living as woman to woman living as woman," in Navajo.

White colored magic emanated from the righthand side of the wheel and flowed upwards like a stream into Stephanie's back. Stephanie felt an unusual sensation and her muscles became more subdued as her body hair disappeared.

"What the hell," she said, looking at her cramping fingers as they became more slender and shorter. Her feet became smaller within her shoes, causing her to yelp at the unsettling changes that were happening to her.

Her nipples filled with milk until they sagged beneath her white shirt. She ran to the bathroom but tripped on her now larger shoes.

"What the fuck is happening to me!" she exclaimed as her voice became higher pitched. His hands moved in front of her mouth as her fat went from the gut to the butt, resulting in a pear-shaped body.

She ached all over her body as she got to the mirror and saw that her face became narrower, sharper, and devoid of any five o'clock shadow. Finally, she could feel her cock and balls receding into a quickly forming envelope with testicles turning into ovaries and a penis turning into a uterus and fallopian tubes. She screamed at the top of her lungs when she felt inside her pants to find a pussy instead of a cock.

Shiladeezi, meanwhile, teleported back to the Albuquerque police headquarters as Stephanie got out her phone and called 911.

"911, what's your emergency?" asked the operator.

"I was turned into a cis woman!" exclaimed Stephanie. "I can't be reassigned like this!"

"What?" asked the operator.

"I was sitting on the couch when I just turned into a cis woman," said Stephanie. "I'm supposed to be gender fluid, not cis!"

"I'm not following... Is this an emergency?" asked the operator.

"You bet your ass it's an emergency, dimwit!" exclaimed Stephanie. "I need a squad to get that motherfucker who made me cis!"

"Alright," said the operator, "we'll send some officers out."

"Perfect!" said Stephanie before the operator hung up, and just one minute later, there was a loud knock on her door, and she immediately walked up to the door and opened it to find two police officers standing at her door.

"You are under arrest for two counts of assault, and anything you say and do, can and will be used against you in a court of law!"

"No, get the guy who made me this way!" demanded Stephanie, quickly backing away from the handcuffs. "Get that motherfucker now!" She ran from the officers around her apartment before the female officer tackled her from behind, holding her down while the male officer applied handcuffs to her wrists. "You can't do this!" she exclaimed after the officers got her up.

"You now have resisting arrest along with the assault allegations. Do you want to make it worse?"

The officers walked out of the apartment as Stephanie exclaimed, "You can't be oppressing me like this! I did what was necessary social justice for the Trans community!"

"Yeah, yeah. Tell it to the judge," he said as the other officer slammed the door shut.

The End

8
TOGETHERNESS

One dark evening in a quiet Rome neighborhood, there was a long stretch of modest looking apartment buildings next to a long, snaking street. They were grey colored and made of concrete, and a black steel fence served as a barrier between the apartments and the outside world. Inside a first story apartment, there was a 15-year-old boy of moderate build with a clean-shaven face and short brown hair sitting miserably at the dining room table. He eyed an array of incomplete math homework staring him in the face. He held a pencil in his left hand while his heavyset mother stood on his right, pouting while looking down upon him with a look of great apprehension.

"Mom," said the boy, "I'm starving, can you please make us some dinner?"

"Not until you do your homework, young man!" argued the Mother

"Mom, I'm not a little kid anymore!" complained the boy. "I'll do it after dinner!"

"Matteo Montalbini Kosinski!" fumed the mother. "I scheduled you to do homework in the hour before dinner, after Francesca and Maria!"

135

"But Mom," said Matteo, "high school work comes from all dir—"

"Shut up and just do your homework!" exclaimed the mother, giving the boy a very strong smack. "I know that it's hard, but the sooner you get it done, the sooner you can go back on Snapchat!"

Matteo promptly got back to doing the remainder of the problems on a sheet of scratch paper. Two preteen girls looked upon their older brother from their bedroom sympathetically.

"Y'know, Francesca," said the taller girl. "It sucks that Mom is starving Matteo like that."

Francesca, the shorter of the two, replied, "Well, at least we don't have to go hiding from her this time."

Matteo, however, concealed his sadness with a flat, melancholy face as his developing stubble flattened with his lip. The girls' frowns turned to smiles once the door opened and revealed their father standing in the door. He was a moderately tall, middle-aged man of stocky build with balding, black hair and a brown paper bag in his right hand.

"Hey Della," he said sheepishly, "I grabbed us dinner."

"And where the fuck were you!" exclaimed Della, shooting a harsh gaze at the father.

"I was working late, and the kids must be starving," said the man as his eyes darted across the room.

"More like you were seeing that skank!" bickered Della, pouting at him. "GIORGIO!"

"We're only friends a-and besides we met at work," said Giorgio.

"I've fucking told you," said Della, pointing at him, "we are married now. You shouldn't be cheating on me like this! Besides,

I gave the kids a schedule that we need to stick to, so just put it in the fridge!"

"Mom!" exclaimed Matteo as Della turned toward him. "I'm 15 now, I don't need this stupid scheduling like Francesca and Maria! Just trust me to do my homework on my own time, like what you did with showering!"

"Alright," said Della, walking towards the counter. "But I still want it done before you go to sleep."

"Okay, Mom," said Matteo as Giorgio put the bag on the counter.

"Girls, it's time for dinner!" announced Della before Maria and Francesca walked up towards the table as Matteo quietly tucked away his notebook and textbook beneath the chair. Giorgio got out several burgers, a few paper containers of French fries, and packets of ketchup. Della raided the fridge for a couple of canned sodas and laid them out at each spot for the kids, placing them on corresponding coasters. All the kids got their burgers and their fries before sitting down on their spots.

Matteo squirted some ketchup from the packet onto the fries as the family ate in awkward silence while scarcely looking up from their plates.

"So, Maria, you did do all of your homework, right?"

Maria quivered for she knew what her mother would do.

"Yes, Mom, I've done all of it."

"Well, that's good," said Della before taking a bite out of her chicken burger.

No one dared to talk at the table, for the tense silence was only broken by the smacking sound of people chewing. Matteo had looked down at his plate, eating his share of fries.

If only there was a way to make us not fight that much, thought Matteo, then an idea came into his head: *If I sneak out and go to the shrine, then I'm sure that the Wizard will do something about it. Now, to get them off my back...* He thought before looking up and saying, "Can I be excused? I'm full."

Della looked him over with a great leer and then to his plate and said, "No Matteo, you need to finish your food!"

Matteo looked down at his dinner with a frown.

"Okay, Mom," he said gleefully.

"People worked hard to make it the way it is, and you need to be respectful of them," stated Della as Giorgio gave a rather coerced nod. Just like that, he went right back to eating, eventually finishing every last morsel that sat on his plate.

"Now, can I be excused please?" he asked with a tone of impatience before Della looked upon him and his plate, saying, "Well, of course, you can, now that you've finished your food."

Matteo soon got up and walked over to the sink before placing his plate in the sink. He promptly walked into his bedroom, which he shared with his sisters, and opened the window sideways. He got a pair of grey sneakers out from under his bed and put them on, quickly tying them. Next, he grabbed his wallet from his bed as well as a pentacle pendant before putting it in his front pocket and his wallet in his back pocket. He got up onto the top bunk of the girl's wooden bunkbed before turning on his back, so his head was on his sister's pillow.

Matteo inched toward the window and planted his feet onto it. Next, he held the side of the bed as his legs soon dangled out of the window over some bushes, like noodles on a fork. He soon bent over and grabbed the black fencepost before pulling himself up over the fence post, falling over onto the sidewalk below.

"UHHH..." said Matteo, grimacing, as he had bruised his back and shoulders. He got up with an intense, dull pain before reaching into his pocket and feeling for the right-facing portion of the five-pointed star. Once he'd done this, he soon closed his eyes and activated the water section of the pentacle by casting magical energy into the pendant. It glowed blue through his pocket, and almost before he knew it, the glowing faded away, for the healing magic had done its job.

He was no longer bruised, so he walked down the street towards Battestini Way, which was a large, three-lane street with cars and motorbikes driving in either direction. He pressed the button to cross the street for on the other side where there was a roofed escalator with a large blue sign reading "Rome Metro" accompanying it. Once he could cross the street, he went straight to the escalator before finding himself in a small line of people standing behind the metro's turnstiles.

People stepped forward inch by inch until Matteo was next, and upon reaching it, he deposited a Euro coin and a 50-cent piece into the turnstile before it spun around, letting him through. He walked onto the station, which smelled heavily of booze and cigarettes as a Satyr street performer played the guitar on one of the benches, stamping his hoof in tune with the music he was playing. A couple of people stopped to give the musician change while others mostly ignored him for the train was already there, the station was the very end of the line. It had its doors open as part of the scheduled stopover. Matteo didn't hesitate to step onto the train and grab the upper handlebar.

Within several minutes, the sliding doors closed, and the train raced away from the station.

The train stopped by a number of stations as people would get on and get off while Matteo stayed on until it got to 3rd Street station in Rome's historical district. He got off and went straight up the escalator, where he was greeted by elaborate stone buildings, basilicas, restaurants, and hotels. He walked down the stone street before he got to a sidewalk where cars had already stopped. On the other side of the street was the Pantheon temple, which had its door wide open.

The temple would be filled with various statues and idols and a large, stone plate in the center of the relatively circular temple with the sculpted faces of six main gods and six main goddesses. The Priest had long left for the night, for the temple was left quiet for people to pray and for local witch covens to perform their magic. There'd be no one here at that hour, for night had just fallen, and the room was dead silent. Matteo grabbed the pendent out of his pocket and kneeled on a large pillow before a section of plate that featured the face of Venus.

He placed the pendant on the plate, making sure the spirit section of the pentacle was pointed toward the center of the plate.

"Oh, mighty Venus, Goddess of Love and Fortune," prayed Matteo as his voice broke up and his eyes closed. The pentacle glowed white as he continued praying, "I propose this humble request: Heal the broken bonds in my family, allow my mother and father to re-enter their sacred union. Let me grow and live. Punish my mother for all the years of abuse, amen." He soon looked up and saw the cock and balls of a nude man out the corner of his eye. "AWW DUDE!" he exclaimed as the pentacle faded back to its normal brass color. "Put some fucking pantss onnn." His gaze soon turned towards the man's dark brown wings with black striations. "Cupid?" he said, walking up to him. "Oh, oh, I'm so sorry for cursing at you, Your Holiness!"

"Don't worry, mortal," consoled Cupid. "I've heard much worse."

"B-but what brings you to this temple?" inquired Matteo, grabbing his pentacle from the plate and placing it back into his front pocket.

"I always check up on my mother's shrines," replied Cupid. "I saw you praying earlier. Is something wrong?"

"Well, ever since my father died in a car crash all those years ago, life has been hell for me!" said Matteo. "My mom won't let me do anything outside of a schedule, and she beats all of us! Me and my sisters are at her mercy. Even my stepdad hasn't helped" He sighed before his voice broke up. "Why is life so unfair? One death, and it's been hell!" He soon began to cry as Cupid gave him a hug and patted him on the back.

"There, there," he said. "I'll be able to help you and your parents."

"Really?" said Matteo with a sniffle "wouldn't you have better things to do as a God?"

"These days I'm only an Angel of Love" said Cupid "But of course, just tell me your address, and I'll see for myself,"

Matteo smiled at the offer.

"You'd do that?"

"It's my duty to," said Cupid. "The Lord still entrusts me with the old duties of being God of Love and Desire, after all."

"If you don't use your arrows," said Matteo, "it's 1230 Battistini Street, Apartment 8."

"Good," said Cupid. "Now, let's go outside, and I can fly you home."

Matteo slowly walked out of the temple before letting Cupid grab him by the chest. Before he knew it, Cupid had launched into the air, and wind gushed by at 50 kilometers an hour. His sadness soon turned to ecstasy as he called out in cheer, for it was a perspective that he had never seen before. Cupid's 4.7-meter wingspan made quick work of the sky, keeping both god and mortal safely in the air.

Once he was back in the neighborhood, Cupid decreased in altitude and got into standing position with his wings, sending great gusts of wind across the street like a giant fan before folding his wings back up, so they resembled a robe.

"I'll be invisible, so I can see what happens, okay?"

"Okay, but give me a boost back into the window since that's where I snuck out of the house from," explained Matteo before Cupid promptly cupped his hands together, so Matteo could step on them to get over the apartment's fencing, so he could crawl back into his room. Once Matteo was in, Cupid shrunk down until he was about the size of a newborn child before seemingly vanishing into thin air and glided through the window before folding his wings back up. He would use repulsion magic to keep him from crashing into the wall or any of the kids. Maria and Francesca sat on Matteo's bed with sad looks on their faces while Della stood in the doorway with her hands on her hips.

"Snuck out again, have we?" said Della. "Avoiding homework, perhaps!"

"No," said Matteo honestly. "I was avoiding you!"

"How dare you avoid your mother!" exclaimed Della. "This is why we have schedules! You can't be trusted with your own time!"

"I'm not a kid anymore!" bickered Matteo

"Matteo Montalbini Kosinski, Go back to homework right now!" commanded Della, walking out of the door frame .

"MOM!" complained Matteo. "You can't do this!"

"Don't make me get the belt!" yelled Della before Matteo shuddered and swiftly walked into the main room, where he got his books and notebook out from beneath the table and proceeded to go right back to doing his homework. Cupid followed them, silently growing in size while still maintaining invisibility.

"For this…escapade, and for lying, you will be grounded," stated Della as Matteo sighed, sitting down.

"Don't you think you're a little harsh?" asked Giorgio, who was watching TV.

"I know what I'm doing. I mean, it's not like you would know anything about lies, right?"

Immediately Giorgio fell silent and resumed his program.

Cupid, meanwhile, had seen enough, so he shrank down again and flew out of the house, gaining normal size and becoming visible again.

What should I do? he wondered, flying over highways. But then he remembered the meeting that the other love gods put together. *That's it! I'll go back to the meeting and ask them take the Montalbinis to the Salmakis Resort, they'll remember their love there!*

Nineteen kilometers away on a vacant beach shore was a temporal Basilica, perceptible only to gods and very powerful Wizards. Venus had called a meeting between herself and the Erotes, as all the gods present were nude and sitting around a long, spectral table.

"Right," said Venus, sitting at the head of the table. "I feel safe about the Kozushis being fused at the Salmakis Resort."

"They may not be praying to us," said Hymen, "but there isn't violence in the household. They just seem to have given up on each other, and I don't see any harm in it."

"A workaholic husband is woefully common in that part of the world," said Hermaphroditus. "Fusing them together should do just the trick."

Hedylogos soon wrote down, "Hiro and Yume Kozushi," on a sheet of enchanted paper on the bottom of a list of other names of couples. Just then, Cupid opened the Basilica door and walked in before swiftly sitting at the nearest vacant spot.

"Ahh, Cupid," said Venus, looking towards him, "has something happened at one of the temples?"

"No, Mom," said Cupid. "I encountered the Montalbinis again by way of their son, and I was considering sending them to the Salmakis Resort."

"Why didn't you use your arrows?" asked Venus. "That's why they're together in the first place, because of your arrows."

The other gods soon looked at Cupid, just as curious as his mother.

"They've lost sincere love," explained Cupid. "You of all gods should know that using the love arrows on two unattracted people would be rape, and God would have my head if I did something that stupid!"

"But either way, I don't think it like is a good idea," said Hermaphroditus. "The fusion of me and Salmacis was merely a means to an end, and I don't think that they would be good as one."

"They had true love when they were married," said Psyche, "so maybe it's not such a bad idea after all."

"Thanks," said Cupid. "The mother is just as bossy as usual, and the dad has virtually given up on parenthood."

"Oh," said Hymen. "If that's how they are, then it just simply cannot happen the way you might think it would be able to happen. It would only result in more animosity in the marriage!"

"Hear me out," said Cupid. "If they wish to remain together, then we'll make it so, but if they want to be apart, then we separate them."

"There's a reason why most souls are separated," argued Hermaphroditus. "It is because people are so different to one another, and the union of two sexes only works out when they're like me, where she wanted freedom," he said, pointing at his left boob, "and he wanted freedom," she said, pointing down to her penis.

"We've had success in fusing couples together in the past!" said Cupid. "A lot of them come to an understanding since their separate thoughts are one united thought."

"Fusion breeds trouble!" argued Hermaphroditus.

"Says the god who got raped by a nymph at 15!" fumed Cupid. "She wouldn't have fused with you if that never happened!"

"First off, I wouldn't have raped him if I hadn't been drafted into Artemis' stupid army!" Fumed Hermaphroditus. "I was dating her in secret, and I had to lie to the other nymphs since the draft meant that we all had to be virgins!"

"Yeah, I've done some crap, too," said Cupid angrily. "But Psyche came in and straightened me out because, if you hadn't noticed, we aren't exactly in an ideal world. Shit happens, and we need to consider all solutions however drastic."

"Now, you see h—" said Hermaphroditus before they and Cupid received a psychic blast from Venus.

"Enough with your pathetic squabbling!" she boomed. "It's your job in this pantheon to be the gods of love and passion. The resort has saved countless of couples from all around the world, and the ones who remain separate still remain together as individual kindred spirits! But if you weren't acting like a bunch of mortal children, you would all know that!"

"So what's the plan now?" said Hymen meekly.

"The plan is that we warp them to the Salmakis Resort in the middle of the night while they are both sleeping," explained Venus, "and then we place them into a room. Is everyone in?"

The other gods looked at each other and wondered about the plan.

"I'm in," stated Cupid.

"I'm in," said Psyche and Hermaphroditus

"I'm in," stated Hedylogos in his natural, deep bassy voice as the other gods brought their hands together.

"Then it's settled," said Venus. "Five more couples to the Salmakis Resort effective tomorrow."

⊱┼⊹⊷⊙⊶⊹┼⊰

Several hours later, all the lights in the Montalbini family apartment were turned off as Giorgio and Della were asleep in the master bedroom. Their alarm clock read 1:30; they were asleep, nice and sound, when Hymen conjured two duplicates of himself in the room while other duplicates were blessing weddings in different parts of the world. The Hymens quietly inched toward the bed and grabbed a hold of them by the back of their necks before he dispelled both selves. The couple would end up in the Time dimension for a split second, encased inside Hymen's sprawling soul.

They soon appeared in the arms of two more Hymens over 1,300 km away from the apartment in Rome. Hedylogos put a sleeping spell on them as the wind and cold air would have knocked them out of sleep. Next, Hermaphroditus stripped them from their pajamas and underwear before placing them in the hotel's fountain. They floated Della closer to Giorgio and cast a merging spell into them, as skin would soon tie the two together. Next, they lined them up on top of each other, so all bones and organs could become one body. Della, being smaller, was pressed onto Giorgio as their heads became one and their bodies became one. She was no longer Della, and he was no longer Giorgio. Now together, they were Diellié.

Hermaphroditus took them out of the fountain and handed them to Venus.

"The spell should wear off in a few hours, given the water and the changes," said Hedylogos before Venus gave a nod and carried them through the main hall and placed them in room 12 once Cupid swiped the corresponding room key into the door and opened it. Venus would carry them into the room before putting them into the bed, tucking them in to the lone queen size bed and walking out of the room, closing the door behind her.

Next morning, Diellié woke up to some odd and very confusing thoughts.

I wonder where Della-Giorgio is? they wondered before their eyes popped out in surprise seeing where they were.

Where are the kids—?

Crap, now how am I supposed to see Rosa if I'm here! they thought.

Wait, her name is Rosa?!

Oh whate—she-me is a giant shrew!

Diellié wanted to talk, but soon thought, *What the hell is going on with my thinking? Who am I or We? What are we? Where are we?*

They would reach their hand down into the sheets before another thought came into their head.

Don't do that. I—or we?—don't know what's going on!

They looked down to see a pair of sagging breasts, and memories of breastfeeding Matteo came to him.

We're an abomination, we're kidnapped, and we don't even know where we fucking are!

They frowned fearfully as memories from both parties came to the other for the first time.

For him, it was memories of Della growing up with Russian immigrants for parents and hearing about the death of her first husband via phone call. For her, it was memories of Giorgio getting bullied in high school and contemplating suicide in a homeless shelter long before he met her. Diellié remained tense and in bed, all the while being too scared to get up or to do much of anything else, so they grabbed the sheets and suffered in silence for the worse part of an hour.

They were starving and getting more scared and confused by the minute until they heard a knock on the door.

"Get the fuck away!" they yelled before grimacing at the odd sound of their voice.

"If I could please come in, I'd like to explain your predicament," said a voice on the other side.

Diellié contemplated the man's words.

"Come in," they said as the door opened, revealing Cupid on the other side.

He walked in, saying, "Now, your oldest son expressed great concern to me that you were, as we say, not the best family around."

Diellié was silent as Cupid walked toward the bed.

"You are at the Salmakis Resort in Turkey, and we fused both of you together into one person, so the physical bond may rekindle what made you romantically attracted to each other in the first place."

Diellié looked at Cupid with a wince, saying, "What are you talking about? We—er I am happy together!"

"Well, judging by what I saw last night, you are a control freak," stated Cupid frankly.

"Am not!" argued Diellié before thinking about Rosa. "Hey, you're right. But I wasn't always like this"

"Maybe it's because something happened in your life," thought Cupid aloud.

"Oh yeah," said Diellié as it hit them. "I started scheduling my kids after my first husband died. I-I scheduled my kids and beat them because I was afraid that I'd lose them as quickly as I lost my husband…" Their voice soon trailed off.

"Very good," said Cupid. "Now go get dressed and join the other couples, the resort has a full continental breakfast."

"I won't have to pay for this, will I?" asked Diellié.

"It's on us," said Cupid

"And one last thing before you leave us be," said Diellié, sitting up in the bed. "How are our kids doing?"

"Great," said Cupid. "I've endowed your son with household authority, but don't worry. He's old enough to start taking care of himself."

Diellié groaned at the loss of control, but soon realized that they needed to learn to be more lenient. Cupid walked out of the room, shutting the door behind him before Diellié got up and walked toward the flat screen TV, which sat on top of a nearby wardrobe. The wardrobe was small and had many drawers, which they rummaged through to find a portion to an outfit in each one. He would experience the foreign feeling of putting on a bra and hooking it together to keep the breasts compressed and well supported, and she would experience the foreign sensation of underpants reaching down past shapely thighs.

They put on a pair of socks, some jeans, and a V-neck before slipping on a pair of sneakers and tying them. They soon walked out of the room and down the hall, where there was classical sculptures and the scent of potato pancakes, beans, and maple syrup wafting in from the dining area. Once they got there, there were several other fused couples, each seemingly speaking a different language as they heard English, Japanese, Zulu, and several other foreign tongues.

They grabbed a plate and got in line behind a fused Orc, who mumbled to themself in Danish. Diellié put two pancakes on their plate before reaching a right hand toward the maple syrup, gagging.

Why am I gagging? thought Diellié.

I don't like syrup, it's disgusting! But I—wait—we're the same person now. Let's just move on... They casually went past the fruit before grabbing a paper bowl and pouring some cereal and then the milk. Finally, they placed a banana next to the pancakes on the main plate as they walked away from the food and sat at an empty table.

They thought about Rosa and how it was his only release between a boring office job and a shrewd wife. This realization hit them like a truck as guilt and deep sadness played in their mind as the tragedy of burying a husband mere weeks after having their youngest daughter truly sank in with them.

We're broken, they thought while eating a mouthful of cereal, sniffling. *How could I be so irrational and withdrawn?* They were brought to tears as they used a napkin to wipe their face.

They started crying while mumbling, "To think that we were so broken that we needed divine intervention." They blew their nose before taking a few bites out of the pancakes. "I was broken," they mumbled, "but, now that I'm together, our quirks should complement each other. I was broken." They soon buttered their pancakes, spreading it thickly. "But now that we're compounded, I'm fixed and complete."

They grinned as they ate their breakfast, thinking about all the goals they wouldn't be able to accomplish were they separate people. As they ate the banana, they daydreamed about investing in the stock market, sending their children to college, and marrying Rosa, so they could have more time to figure out themself.

They were so lost in thoughts that almost before they knew it, they had finished all of their breakfast.

I wonder if I should shower now. I must be stinky, and it would be good to figure out my body, they thought, stroking their chin. Anteros walked into the room with stacks of Lira bills that he placed on each table as each person had their stack of 1,000 Turkish Lire given to them. Diellié watched as others were given money before Anteros walked right up to their table, giving them a stack of money.

"Here's some spending money for you to understand yourself," he said.

"Thanks," they said humbly, "but we won't be able to use this back home."

"The resort is near a town called Bodrum, and it has plenty of shops. The money is for spending, so you can see what you like or not, if it makes any sense to you," explained Anteros

"I know what you mean," said Diellié as they got up and put the money in their back pocket. "Now, do you think I should shower since I'm going out, or…?"

"The spell that we cast that brought you together also cleaned your being," said Anteros. "You shouldn't worry about that too much"

"Good," said Diellié, getting up and setting the bowl on top of the plate and walking over to the nearest garbage can.

"Now, when you want to come back home, come back to the resort this evening. We'll have a portal bringing everyone home, understood?" asked Anteros.

"But what if I get lost?" asked Diellié worriedly. "I've never been to Turkey before."

"Bodrum is small enough where you should know your way around," eased Anteros.

"Thanks," replied Diellié. "I'll see you later."

"You too," said Anteros as they walked out of the dining hall through the lobby and out the front door.

They were stunned at Bodrum's scenery, as it was a beautiful beachside town where the weather was warm, the beaches were white, and sky was blue. They would go on numerous escapades buying shirts, a couple of keychains, and a rug. They took in the sights, had some lunch, and spent a good couple of hours combing the beaches. The town seemed idyllic to them, and despite occasional stares from locals, they had discovered themself in a way that wouldn't be possible otherwise.

That evening as the sun came down in the sky, there was a portal where Cupid asked the couples whether or not they wanted to be separated. Most were separated by Hermaphroditus at the cost of their clothes before going through the portal to their house as two, while some others remained together going through as one.

"So," said Cupid. "Given how depressed you were earlier, I would assume you'd like to be separated."

"I'd like to remain together," said Diellié. "I'm better off like this than I would be separated. Besides I could marry the girl of my dreams without cheating."

"But you two were so different," said Hermaphroditus.

"That was before I understood how similar we really are and how together as man and woman, we are whole," said Diellié. "So I'd rather be together."

"Well, have a good day," said Hermaphroditus.

"You too," replied Diellié before stepping into the portal with their hands full of shopping bags. They came out of the other end standing tall and confident in their own apartment as the portal closed behind them.

Crap, thought Diellié. *I had work today, but on the other hand Cupid or whoever probably told them in advance.* They soon sat down on the couch and turned on the TV for the first time as one.

Just 30 minutes later, a door opened.

"Mom, you're back!" said Francesca as Diellié turned their head. "Or Dad…?" said Francesca, confused at their plump yet sharp face.

"Kids, I'm no longer your mother, nor your father," said Diellié. "Ever since the gods fused us in Turkey, we've been whole."

"Well, what are we supposed to call you then?" asked Maria as Matteo remained speechless, for he didn't expect the gods to answer his prayer like this.

"I am now your parent, but you can call me either Mom or Dad when it's comfortable, but things are going to be different," they said.

"In what ways?" asked Matteo, shaky on what to call them.

"As much as it pains me to say this, there is no more schedule," said Diellié. "But if any of you misbehave, you'll go right back onto the schedule."

The daughters gasped, for a great weight had been lifted from their shoulders.

"And Matteo," said Diellié. "You are no longer grounded. Your sneaking out of the house is the best thing to happen to me. But now that things have changed, don't do that again."

"I won't," said Matteo as Diellié sat back on the couch with their feet pointed upwards.

"Well," said Matteo, turning to his sisters. "Go do your homework."

Maria and Francesca walked towards the kitchen table and set their backpacks down, for they were already so used to the schedule. Matteo, meanwhile, walked into the bedroom and laid down on his bed.

Diellié, now being one, went on to continue Giorgio's old job accounting in a telemarketing firm, and they were gone from the home for much of the day. This left Matteo in charge of his sisters for much of the day, giving them newfound freedom to live their lives. Every other day was spent either at friend's houses, temples, or around town doing work in local libraries and coffee houses.

The uncanniness of their parent was strange for them to witness, as whenever Diellié was home, the kids would be in their bedroom or around town from the strange being they called 'Mom' or 'Dad.' This continued for a week until they were fully comfortable with having a single, hermaphrodite parent. Rosa shared the aversion at first, but soon warmed up to them after they explained what had happened and their experiences in Bodrum.

As Rosa became more acquainted with Diellié, they got more comfortable dating again. After a while, she became a familiar face in the Montalbini family apartment, and they all lived happily sometimes after.

The End

9
THE TROUBLED WITCH DOCTOR

In a remote Congolese jungle surrounded by towering mahogany trees was a small mud hut with a thatched straw roof. The hut itself was rather bare on the inside save for a fire pit, an array of large towels, a lawn chair and a black 30 cm cathode ray TV sat on top of a small wooden table. There was also a shelf in the back of the hut that featured empty plastic bottles, stone bowls, spell books, and various enchanting ingredients. The walls were a dull, brownish grey with its only decorations being a small white wooden idol of a nude, long-bodied woman with a large head, a few abstract looking wooden masks and a framed white medical degree sitting prominently on the opposite end of the TV.

"This certification from the University of Kinshasa," read the degree in French, "hereby permits Dr. Jean Masambo license to practice medicine." The Doctor could be seen with large, poofy white hair and a wrinkled, clean-shaven face. He sat down in a lawn chair in front of the TV while his large, curly magic staff rested against the arm of the chair. He used the TV to divine an image of the dirt access road that snaked its way through the jungle despite the hut's lack of electricity. He looked upon the screen in deep concentration as a compact sedan slowly came into view before driving offscreen.

The man broke his concentration, causing the TV to turn off before he grabbed his stick and got himself up out of the chair. He folded the chair and rested it against the hut's wall and walked out of an opening in the hut as the sedan stopped and parked next to his pickup. The car's door opened, and out came a wiry young dwarf who walked out of the car with a limp, closing the door behind her.

"Ah, Miss Mapunya," greeted Jean. "What brings you out here?"

"Well, Doctor," said Ms. Mapunya, limping into the hut. "I've got these warts on my feet, and they've been bothering me."

"Hmm," said the Doctor following the patient. "Now, when did you first notice this?"

"Just last Tuesday," said Ms. Mapunya, lying down on one of the towels. "I just noticed these white patches on the bottom of my feet, and they've been getting more painful by the day!"

"Well, why don't you take off your shoes, and I'll see what I can do about it," said the Doctor as Ms. Mapunya took her sneakers off and set them aside.

Jean picked up his staff and walked towards the shelf, grabbing a bottle and some herbs.

"You are going to give me some solution for this, right?" asked Ms. Mapunya.

"Of course, madam," replied Jean, walking back to where she lay. "I know exactly what to do." He set the herbs aside as he flipped open the spell book to find the right spell that corresponded to the ailment. It was about a minute before he got to the middle of the page. "O all the unseen forces descent from the of the great Nzambi a Mpuungu," he chanted before singing: "Heal this poor woman of her ills and rid the body of Demons and ancestors!" He danced and shuffled in accordance to the magic that was flowing in from the unseen dimension to Jean's body.

His staff glowed red as he rubbed it by Ms. Mapunya's feet as the red magic traveled out of the staff and into her feet. The bunions shrank down to the point of vanishing as the staff's magic faded away, revealing its usual color underneath a flowing ruby veneer. With the remaining magic, Jean placed a bowl full of water into the bottle, completely filling it. Next, he dropped the herbs in before draining the staff's magic into the water.

The herbs disintegrated, and the water became lukewarm while turning into a deep mustard color, and the staff turned back into its usual brown and black wood pattern. Jean walked over to the shelf and grabbed a large, white lid, screwing it on giving it the appearance of liquid cough syrup. Ms. Mapunya put her shoes on and gasped at the lack of pain.

"Thank you," she said. "I don't know what I would've done without you."

"It's no problem," said Jean, handing her the healing potion. "This solution will help you any time you have pain. For everything that I've done from the healing to the solution, that will be 32,000 Franc please." Jean held out his hand as Ms. Mapunya reached into her purse and pulled out a 20,000, a 10,000, and two 1,000 Franc bills before putting them in Jean's hand. "Thank you very much," he said walking out of the hut. "I've got to do something in town, so I'll be seeing you."

"Ah, Nzuzi," said Jean with a smile. "So how was school?"

"It was awful," replied Nzuzi. "I showed all the kids my phone that you gave me, and now, they're all mean to me for some reason."

"Well," said Jean, driving away, "they're probably just jealous. I mean there's a lot of kids around here who don't have a TV or even electricity."

"Their mommies and daddies sound mean," stated Nzuzi.

"You are very lucky to have that phone," stated Jean. "A lot of people can't afford these things. They're too poor, so you shouldn't take these things for granted."

"I know, Grandpa!" exclaimed Nzuzi. "You always talk about this!"

"But it's true," stated Jean frankly. "Boy, when I was your age, we didn't have much of anything to brag about. Everyone was without power and shoes under Belgian rule. We didn't brag about anything because we had nothing to brag about. You see, we were happy then because we had to make the most of what little we had. We understood each other and we played with each other because of it. What I'm trying to say is that a little humility goes a long way. Perhaps next time you might let other kids play with your phone."

Nzuzi had long tuned out his ranting grandfather as he looked out the window at churches, single-story concrete buildings, and haphazardly made powerlines that lay taught above a large network of dirt streets. They got to their house on the edge of town. It was grey colored and had a tin roof with a large TV antenna topping it, like a stringy, metal chimney. It resembled most of all the other houses in the neighborhood save for a small shed in the backyard that laid flush against the righthand side of the neighbor's brown picket fence.

"Well," said Jean, parking his truck in front of the house. "I hope our talk meant something."

"Yes, Grandpa," replied Nzuzi, getting out of the passenger side door before running up the street. Jean, meanwhile, turned off the truck and got out via the driver's side door before closing it, putting the key in its keyhole and locking it. He paced up onto the front yard toward the simple wooden door and opened it to a large, simple room with a carpeted floor, a gas stove, a dining table, & a modest leather sofa where his daughter-in-law could be seen watching TV.

"Jean," she said turning off the 70 cm flat screen TV, which sat on at the house's front wall by the door. "We need to talk."

"Has that Priest been bothering you again, Bompaka?" asked Jean.

"What? No!" exclaimed Bompaka. "I worry that Nzuzi won't be able to control his powers."

"What are you talking about?" asked Jean. "He doesn't have any powers, and he can't inherit them anyways!"

"What if I told you that he's been wetting the bed?" stated Bompaka.

"But that doesn't necessarily mean he has dark energy to empty," explained Jean. "That could be for a number of reasons. And besides, Kalunga—nor any of my kids—seemed to inherit my powers, so why would Nzuzi?"

"Well, genes do skip generations, right?" asked Bompaka.

"Yes, of course, they do," said Jean. "But that is a recessive gene, and the Gods made that gene as rare as one that would give someone a sixth finger!"

"But he's been wetting the bed ten nights in a row!" she argued.

"I'll tell you what," he said. "Don't give him any water before bed, and if he still wets the bed, then have a good talk to him about magic."

"That sounds good," she replied. "I'll definitely try that tonight and see what happens."

That evening, at the Idiofa police precinct, two officers sat at a table in a simple break room with grey stone walls and a grey carpeted floor to match.

"You know something?" asked Officer Gzenga, sipping his coffee. "Whenever something bad happens, it always seems to happen after a Witch hunt."

"You're crazy," smirked Officer Botende. "You surely don't think that they're jinxing everyone in town, now."

"No, but think about this," stated Officer Gzenga, pointing at the air. "When we almost busted that coven by Shimba last week, my little cousin caught AIDS."

"There's no way they would put a curse on her," said Officer Botende. "They hardly know you."

"The Devil controls people like that," explained Officer Gzenga. "I read somewhere that magic involves demonic posession, Satan's probably controlling them."

"So what?" shrugged Officer Botende. "That's why we bust Witches, so what does it matter that bad things keep happening?"

"Year after year, everything is going to shit!" said Officer Gzenga. "There's more chaos now than ever before! It may start with witchcraft, but it always ends in wickedness!"

"Hm…" pondered Officer Botende, thinking about what his partner had said. "Maybe you've got a point." The brown, wooden door opened, and in came the Chief, who was a short, stout man in a decorated uniform.

"Gentlemen," said the Chief "Father Mosatu is in the interrogation room with a divine tip."

"Well, sir," said Officer Botende before walking out with Officer Gzenga, "we'll see what he has to say."

The precinct was a simple building with a waiting area and a short hallway with doors leading to offices and two interrogation rooms. Officer Botende opened the door to another simple room with a white table and two chairs. Sitting on the other end was a tall man in a white bishop's robe with yellow lining and a staff topped by a golden cross in his right hand.

"Father," said Officer Gzenga as Officer Botende shut the door behind them. "What do you know about the Witch Doctor problem around here?"

"Well," said Father Mosatu, "our Father in Heaven told me that he is just outside of Kibuge Village in the middle of some trees."

"Do you have any exact coordinates?" asked Officer Gzenga.

"The coven lies at 4.8 degrees south, 19.8 degrees east," said Father Mosatu as Officer Botende wrote down the coordinates on his notepad. "But before you go out on the witch hunt, you will need a crucifix and a radio."

"That won't be any problem," said Officer Gzenga, pulling out a small, battery-powered radio. "We always keep this when we go out on patrol."

"Then you are aware that both divine and satanic power always create interference on the lower bands, right?" asked Father Mosatu.

"Y-yes, of course, Father," said Officer Gzenga. "Low and medium frequency."

"Well, it sounds like you've got it then," stated Father Mosatu. "Now, just go out on patrol and bring these Witch Doctors to me!"

"Wouldn't that be overstepping the law though?" asked Officer Botende.

"The Chief has already granted me exclusive permission to exorcise and cleanse these witches of corrupt energy," said Father Mosatu. "So what are you waiting for? Bring me that coven!"

"Y-yes, Father," said Officer Gzenga, getting up as Officer Botende opened and went out the door. "Thank you very much for the intel."

"It's my divine service," said Father Mosatu humbly. "I'm always happy to help."

The officers walked out of the room, closing the door behind them before walking down the hall toward the precinct's main entrance. Officer Botende ripped off the paper with the coordinates before leaving the rest of the notepad on the counter. They walked toward the patrol car as Officer Gzenga stepped into the driver's seat while Officer Botende got into the passenger seat.

"Ya ready?" asked Officer Botende, getting out a wooden crucifix from the cruiser's glove box.

"Of course," answered Officer Gzenga, turning on the cruiser engine. "Just turn on the radio, and we'll see where they are!"

Officer Botende would do just that before tuning into a talk station with a relatively strong signal save for some faint whistling noises in the background as they drove through town.

It was a bright, full moon night as the dirt street waved its way past small villages while Officer Botende stared at the map on his phone that had a virtual pin on top of the prophesized coordinates. He only had the phone on intermittently, as its electrical interference caused mild, low-pitched buzzing to take over the frequency. With the phone powered off, the station would come in with more relative clarity, breaking what would otherwise be dead silence apart from the cruiser's engine.

The officer's prior experience with witch hunts resulted in everything from an officer's death by decapitation to a catastrophic forest fire. They had to be prepared for anything and everything that could happen at the hunt. As they came closer & closer to the coordinates, a loud buzzing took over the frequency with nothing left of the station that had come in prior. The buzzing was loud and came with a chittering sound that resembled that of a woodpecker. Officer Botende quickly got out his phone and saw how close they were to the on-screen pin.

"That road, it leads right to their coven," he said, pointing at the nearby access road before Officer Gzenga turned on the sirens and meandered his way through the road.

Meanwhile, down the road, there was a hut with a brilliant red light emanating from within. Jean and his fellow coven of Humans, Vampires and Orks had been chanting, "Mandoka, come here to replenish our supplies and our magic. We, the healers of Kwilu, conjure your aura to this point to assist us in our goal to alleviate suffering," while they all danced around a roaring fire pit wearing wooden masks. There was also a pile of various items laying before the fireplace while their leader, an ancient Fairy named Mandoka lead the ritual from the top of the idol that served as a flattering caricature of her appearence.

She first directed the magic into some plastic potion bottles to revitalize their respective effects be it healing or conjury. All their staffs lay on top of the bottles like heavily skewed chimneys, as they would've been regenerated by the same magic that regenerated the potions. Before Mandoka could say anything else, the blaring sound of police sirens and the appearance of blue and red lights come in from outside.

The masked Witches stopped dancing as Mandoka frantically ran toward the magic energy and flew inside of it. Her wings stopped beating as she floated inside it like an ice cube in water. She spread her body outward and radiated the red magic, so that it surrounded the hut like a translucent cocoon.

"O, powerful Obambo," she sang out. "Take us far away to a place where we won't be detained!"

The hut and its occupants seemingly vanished into thin air by the time the Officers got there. There was a cloud of crimson mist that gradually disappeared into nothing, and the radio gradually resumed to the station that it had been receiving earlier.

"Where did they go?" asked Officer Botende with a wide, open gaze while the mist dissipated into nothing.

"Only God knows now," said Officer Gzenga. "Now turn it off, they're probably out of our jurisdiction anyways."

The hut was now over 300 km away in the dense forest of the Salong National Park in Mai-Ndombe. Mandoka flitted down to the ground to catch her breath.

"Hey!" exclaimed one of the Witches drawing his fangs. "What the hell was that?!"

"We couldn't even enchant our TVs with unbreaking!" complained another, pointing at a large dent on a TV's left speaker grille.

"I got us out of Kwilu!" exclaimed Mandoka "You all must've noticed that there were police on our road who would've had us arrested!"

"Well, our apologies, Mandoka," said Jean, "but this used up most of our free magic!"

"Well, I assume you all don't want to be rotting in prison!" exclaimed Mandoka.

"Fair enough," muttered a tusked Witch.

"I've helped you for over 50 years now, and we can't keep running away like this!" she exclaimed, flying in front of Jean's face and pointing at him.

"Well, what do you think we should do?" argued Jean. "For as long as the Catholic missions have been here, the church has always made us seem evil."

"Some of us are monsters as well," stated a Vampire "As a natural predator, they have a right to be afraid of someone like me, but at the same time, I can't help it!"

"It's been passed down from generation to generation," remarked a Human. "There would be no point in convincing them at this stage."

"Well, I propose that we start taming dragons!" suggested Mandoka. "Let's target the church and the government to really hold them accountable."

There was an audible gasp.

"But last time we did that," said Jean, "we caused a civil war to break out, and nothing improved since then, hell, there's still covens fighting for recognition and rights over in Kasaï; and if you ask me, that's only made us look worse!"

"What else is there?" asked Mandoka. "Just let the 'holier than thou' clergy and nepotistic politicians persecute us at every step?"

"That will do nothing but convince them that we're psychotic lunatics!" argued Jean. "If we state our objections civilly, then they would be more kind to listen to us!"

"That would work if they were willing to listen," said an Ork "but they already think that we're evil, despite our otherwise charitable work."

"Besides," said Mandoka, "would most people believe the man who fed, clothed, and taught them or would they believe us felons who are under my supposedly dark spell?"

"I see," said Jean. "Bu—"

"But nothing!" interrupted Mandoka. "In all my millennia, I've seen all kinds of wickedness throughout this land, and in all that time, the most effective evils are the ones who pretend to be good. To show people the government's wickedness, we need a call to arms, so people can really see just how terrible they are. I mean, if you were a zebra letting a pride of lions tell you where to graze, what would you do?"

"R-resist," said Jean nervously.

"Precisely," replied Mandoka.

"There's nothing left to lose," shrugged a Human. "We're already evil in their eyes. We'd only get more sympathizers, too."

"Then it's settled!" said Mandoka. "Sometime this week, we will launch an assault on the church and the state. Now, teleport back to your homes, and we'll deal with this as soon as possible."

Each of the coven members nodded and grabbed their staffs, which glowed brightly before they each vanished into thin air.

"Jean," said Mandoka, as he was the only one who hadn't vanished, "I know you're not a fan of violence, but what else really is there?"

"Fair enough," said Jean. "It is high time some alternatives to charities and Doctors got some notice."

"Well, have a good evening," said Mandoka.

"You too!" said Jean, grabbing his staff and letting it glow sky blue as the world around him turned black before the sight of his living room and the whole family watching TV came into view. Everything went black again as Jean passed out and fell backwards with a loud thud.

The family jumped in their seat at the noise.

"What was that!" exclaimed Nzuzi as Kalunga looked back at his father, who lay stiff in the middle of the room.

"Dad?" he asked worried, as they all got up off the couch and walked toward where Jean lay until they each stood over him.

"Dad?" asked Nzuzi. "Is Grandpa dead?"

"Well, let's see…" replied Kalunga, getting down on his knees and clasping his fingers around Jean's left wrist. "Well, there's still a pulse," he stated.

"He can't keep living like this!" said Bompaka. "All the magic will catch up to him."

"But Grandpa said that magic makes you live forever," said Nzuzi, looking up at his Mother.

"Only if you know how to cope with it," explained Kalunga. "If you cast a spell that your body can't withstand, it drains all of your spirit, and you just faint."

"Really?" said Nzuzi.

"When your uncle, Kivuvu, was being trained to do witchcraft," explained Kalunga, "he would always come home passed out, but now it seems age has caught up to him." He let go of the wrist before he got up and turned toward his wife, saying, "Let's put him on the couch, so he'll get up more easily."

"But I'm not going to pass out when Grandpa starts training me," said Nzuzi, thinking about his father's words, "am I?"

"I don't think so," said Bompaka, putting her arms beneath Jean's armpits. "You'd just feel tired after doing the magic." She lifted one end, and he lifted the other as they both carried Jean onto the couch.

"Why?" asked Nzuzi.

Once they laid him on the couch with his squat nose up toward the ceiling, Bompaka replied, "I'll tell you when you're older. You're not ready to handle the truth yet."

"But Mom!" said Nzuzi.

"No buts," replied the mother. "It's almost bedtime, anyways."

"Well, can I have my water then?" asked Nzuzi.

"I don't think so," said Bompaka. "You've been wetting the bed too much."

"But sweetheart, what might that have to do with anything?" asked Kalunga before Bompaka leaned in and whispered something in his ear. "Oh," he said. "Well, you heard your mother. Go brush your teeth and get ready for bed."

"Okay Dad," said Nzuzi begrudgingly before walking down to the end of the room and opening the door to the bathroom, closing it behind him.

Jean would wake up about ten hours later with a throbbing headache as it had been daylight by that time. He cringed in pain as he rubbed his forehead with his left hand. *Time to check up on Nzuzi,* thought Jean noisily as he rolled over so that his feet dangled beyond the couch. He soon got up to a sitting position, placing his hand on one of the cushions before getting up into a standing position.

He walked toward the back of the room, still feeling somewhat dizzy before he opened Nsuzi's bedroom door and stepped inside. Jean was aghast to see a large, wet stain near dead center of the blanket, so he briskly walked out of the bedroom and over to the kitchen counter. There was a notepad lying next to a glass cup with an assortment of pencils and pens sticking out, like a bed of spikes. He took a pen from the cup and wrote down: "Ask him if he feels any different from normal." After having eaten a small breakfast, he walked out of the house and turned on his pickup just as Bompaka got up out of bed.

After Bompaka showered and brushed her teeth, she went to the kitchen and made breakfast for the whole family while Kalunga walked into Nzuzi's room. He was taken aback by the giant wet spot where Nzuzi had been sleeping. His eyes went wide as his shaking hand caressed the top blanket.

"N-Nzuzi," he said nervously, rubbing his son. "Time to get up." Nzuzi groaned and yawned before opening his eyes while his wincing father said, "You g-gotta go to school, so get dressed and brush your teeth." Kalunga swiftly walked out of Nzuzi's bedroom and back out into the kitchen.

"Honey," said Kalunga, pouring cereal into the wooden bowl. "Nzuzi wet the bed."

Bompaka's jaw dropped.

"What are we gonna do?" she asked as he poured milk into the bowl.

"We just can't keep him home!" said Kalunga. "He'll freak!"

"Has Jean left a note?" asked Bompaka.

"Should be right on the counter," said Kalunga, gingerly putting the cereal on the table.

Bompaka picked it up and read it as Kalunga sat down for scrambled eggs.

"I say we still send him," stated Kalunga. "We still want him to have an education, and we can even afford it all right through to high school."

"I'll talk with him when he comes out," said Bompaka.

"Sounds good," replied Kalunga as the shower turned off.

"Have a good day at work," said Bompaka as Kalunga put on his tie and tightened it around his neck.

"You too," replied Kalunga as he walked out the door, shutting it behind him.

Bompaka gingerly placed Nzuzi's breakfast on the table, careful not to spill anything as he came down to the table mere minutes later.

"Mom?" asked Nzuzi "Where did Dad go?"

"He's off to work," replied Bompaka. "Now, eat your breakfast"

"Now, why has he been acting so weird?" asked Nzuzi.

"Now, let me tell you something," stated Bompaka frankly. "It seems you've inherited your grandpa's powers, and we worry that you won't be able to control it!"

"But Mom, I don't feel any different," yawned Nzuzi

"Well, it's good to hear that, but you can't use any magic out at school," said Bompaka. "We don't want you to be in trouble with the police, now would we?"

"No, Ma," said Nzuzi, recalling how Father Mosatu preached in his classroom about Witches & idolatry.

"Good, now wipe your face," said Bompaka, pointing to Nzuzi's milk moustache. He did so as they walked out of the house and towards his mother's car. She got in on the driver's side, and he got in on the passenger's side and buckled up before he closed the door. "Now, I don't want you using magic at any time at school today, even if it's for healing. The cops are going to be all over you like they are with Grandpa."

"Well, that's stupid!" exclaimed Nzuzi. "Like, they act like it's bad, but why is it, like, bad?"

"I'll tell you when you're older," said Bompaka, driving up to the school. "Now remember, no magic at any time!"

"I know, Ma," he said, rolling his eyes.

"Good," replied Bompaka. "Just wanted to make sure. Now, have a good day at school."

"Bye, Mom," said Nzuzi, getting out of the car as Bompaka shut the driver's side door and drove off. Nzuzi played on the playground as usual until the bell rang, and all the kids ran off into their classrooms. They each sat down in their assigned desk and obtained their books and notebooks from a small cubby that was built into the bottom of the desk.

"Good morning," said the teacher, getting markers out of a Tupperware box and writing the schedule on the board. "So today we're going to learn about spelling, then math, and then we'll have recess. After that, we'll read history and then you turn in your homework before PE. Then you'll have lunch, and finally, you will look at the science of the weather."

After the teacher had taken roll, Nzuzi nodded off, for he felt very tired while the teacher rambled about spelling and the Kongo alphabet while writing letters with diacritics on the whiteboard. He had his notebook opened, but he seldom wrote anything else.

Everyone is just so mean, he thought. *Magic isn't bad…they are! Why can they be mean, but I can't!*

"Nzuzi!" said the teacher as she stood over his desk. "You're not writing the word 'calendar' like I told you to!"

"What is even the point!" exclaimed Nzuzi as electric sparks flashed between his fingers. "You're all mean, so you get in trouble like we do!"

"Nzuzi Masambo!" exclaimed the teacher. "I don't know where this is coming from, but you are going to the principal's office!"

Nzuzi hit the teacher with lightning magic, and she immediately seized, and her skin developed severe burns before she fell to the ground as other students aghast and speechless at what he was doing.

"I don't want Grandpa to be in trouble!" he screamed as even more magic came out of his fingers and arms. The whiteboard was blanked out as the lights rapidly flickered on and off, and the teacher's comatose corpse was tossed around the room like a ragdoll as the other students cowered under their desks.

Nzuzi emitted a telekinetic pulse that saw desks and other items falling over as a few of his peers were crushed by their own desks. The sound of sirens could be heard from outside of the building as the lights sparked and burned out due to Nzuzi's power surge. An older teacher opened up the door as Officers Gzenga and Botende ran into the room and promptly tackled Nzuzi to the ground.

"You're coming with us, kid!" said Officer Gzenga as he put sacramental handcuffs on his wrists. "Think you could fool us, foul Witch!"

Meanwhile, Jean had been watching the whole thing on the TV in his hut as eyes were wide open. He defocused his magic as the TV turned off.

"I'm coming for you!" he said as he got up from his chair and grabbed his magic staff as well as a spell book off the shelf, and walked out of the hut and into the woods. He swiftly walked past trees and through dense thicket before he came across a great flightless dragon with many brown and blue colored feathers as she lay resting on the forest ground. Jean walked beside her before the dragon turned her long neck toward Jean, bearing her razor sharp teeth before she preceded to growl in his face.

"You will be tame to me and under my control," chanted Jean as his staff glowed blue, and he charged up his power. "I am man, and you are beast, and you serve me as I serve the Gods." A beam of baby blue light went into the dragon's green eyes, putting her under hypnosis as blue magic flowed out of his staff back into the surrounding air. He scaled the dragon and straddled her back while wheezing as many feathers brushed up against his blue jeans. He grabbed the base of the dragon's neck and began to steer her through the jungle.

Later, Nzuzi remained in cuffs as he was escorted through the halls of the police precinct by the officers and put into the interrogation room.

I don't wanna go to jail!" screamed Nzuzi. "I didn't do anything wrong, so I don't need to be in trouble!"

In the interrogation room, Father Mosatu stood on the other side of the room wearing a black robe with a crucifix in his right hand and a switchblade in his left.

"Boy, it seems Demons have gotten into you," said Father Mosatu as Nzuzi sat where he was while crying. "I know exactly how to knock the sin out of you."

"I don't care about sin," sobbed Nzuzi. "I just don't want Grandpa to die!"

"You see," said the Priest, "your grandfather is a wicked man who was tempted by the Devil!"

"You're wrong!" exclaimed Nzuzi "My Grandpa is very nice, and he helps a lot of people to feel better!"

"It seems your grandfather lied to you," said the Priest, and he gave a plastic grin. "He doesn't help the sick, he only helps Satan and his minions. He is a very corrupt man, and it seems that you inherited his corruption, looks like I'll have to exorcize the Demons from your body."

"Excer—what!"

"Hold him down!" exclaimed the Priest as the two policemen grabbed their arms around Nzuzi as he screamed: "WHAT ARE YOU GONNA DO TO ME!"

"Our Father in Heaven," chanted the priest in Latin. "Extract the wickedness and magic from this boy's body!" He soon slit Nzuzi's arms with a switchblade as he screamed out in pain. "Release the wickedness from him, so he doesn't follow the satanic path of witchcraft!" He punched Nzuzi square in the face before getting out a small thermos of holy water and pouring it on his wounds. "The power of Christ compels you!" he exclaimed, violently shaking the boy against the officers' grip.

"Stop!' exclaimed Nzuzi before the Priest preceded to repeatedly punch and slap him on the chest and stomach.

"THE POWER OF CHRIST COMPELS YOU!" he said, flinging holy water on Nzuzi as a loud, rumbling roar came from outside. He squished the back of his neck and kept shaking him. "Out of this poor young boy and descend back to the pits of hell!"

The wall on the lefthand side came off as a bestial maw came through the room. The dragon screeched at the humans as the rest of the wall collapsed and crumbled. When the smoke cleared, Nzuzi saw his grandfather riding on the dragon's back as well as an angry mob of rioters.

The rioters were armed with everything from rakes and torches to steel pipes and pistols.

"You have no right to command God's creation!" complained a rioter, digging his rake into the dragon's hide.

"You can't just be going around destroying our town!" protested another as the officers let go of Nzuzi as Father Mosatu ran out the side of the building toward the mob with Nzuzi running out behind him.

"He's getting away!" exclaimed an officer.

"What?" said Father Mosatu, turning around to find Nzuzi and holding him up. "This is a witch child! He is the grandson of the Witch; he has inherited his corruption, and it would be justified to put his grandfather to death and for the boy to be shunned!"

"You might think me corrupt, but I'm here for the boy!" exclaimed Jean. "So hand him over!"

"His exorcism isn't complete. His magic comes from Satan and his Demons!" exclaimed Father Mosatu. "He's corrupted by evil, as you have been, so I advise the both of you, let Jesus into your hearts, so you can make it to heaven!"

Jean had the dragon rear her head as she knocked over the Priest as well as a few rioters. She stepped toward the mob as rakes and pipes cut away at her feathers, revealing callous, grey scales.

"Come on up here, Nzuzi!" he exclaimed, reaching a hand down by the dragon's belly. Nzuzi got up despite feeling feint and grabbed his grandfather's wrinkled hand as Jean put his hand beneath Nzuzi's butt to give him a boost, and both were now on the back of the dragon despite the mob jeering them.

One moment, they could be plainly seen hugging each other, and the next, they vanished into thin air, reappearing a hundred kilometers away in the savannah as Nzuzi developed further slash marks on his clothes and his skin. He screamed in pain as Jean fell backwards with his arms hardly moving.

"Make me better, Grandpa!" said Nzuzi, looking down at Jean's unmoving face. "G-Grandpa?" he asked as Jean lacked a pulse and his eyes remained wide open, as if a three-headed monster invaded his house. "Grandpa?" he said before sobbing and sniffling over Jean's freshly deceased corpse. He hugged it as if it were alive, and he wept into his chest.

"Here lies Dr. Jean Masambo," read his tombstone, "11th of September, 1941 – 26th of March, 2019, a General Practitioner who was a long time Witch, misled by Satan and loved by all who he had conned." The rest of the coven had been arrested, as Father Mosatu prohibited the funeral from taking place as part of the hunt.

Bompaka wept in the doorframe, blowing her nose on a red dish rag, as she wasn't allowed to care for her son ever again. Nzuzi was left to wander the streets as the witch trial called for the whole town to shun him because of his magic powers. Everyone in the neighborhood shut their doors and locked them at Nzuzi's mere presence. With nowhere else to go, he was left to wander the streets out of town and into the savannah.

The End

10
THE POWER OF INSELF

One sunny November day on a spacious ranch in India where mango trees grew and cattle peacefully roamed the yellowing pasture, a ranch house had a small satellite dish jutting out from the roof. Inside, the hot sun beat down from the front windows as an affluent Naga named Shiv Jasim, the wife of Mayor Yaj Sivadi coiled round a small plastic bin that she'd been using as a nest. There, an assortment of eggs had been incubating for the past several months. Shiv, meanwhile, had laid back on her tail and read an array of magazines that had piled up on her coffee table while a cop show was being played in the background.

There was a small, shaking sound, and Shiv grinned with delight, so she slithered toward the cordless phone and pressed a few buttons on its keypad. She held it up to her ear and waited for the dial tone to stop.

"Dharmapuri City Hall, Mayor Yaj Sivadi speaking," said a voice on the other end.

"Honey," said Shiv. "Come quick, they're hatching!"

"Really?" said Yaj happily. "I'll have my Mage warp me there as soon as possible. I'll be there in a few minutes."

"Great, bye," said Shiv before Yaj hung up on the other end. She slithered back to watch as the spotted eggs went crick-crack with a couple even rolling around within the nest. She pointed the remote at the TV, and turned it off before she slithered toward a set of drawers where there was a fanny pack and a rotund black camera.

She went back to the nest to find that the eggs developed even more cracks, and within a few moments, Yaj was in the room. Shiv turned around to witness the sight of her husband.

"Honey, you're just in time!" she said happily as he slithered over to the nest.

"Wow," said Yaj, watching them while interlocking his tail with his wife's "Thank the Gods, I'm a father."

A tiny hand poked out of the egg as the two watched in amazement. The egg cracked more, revealing the pudgy torso of a Naga baby with a callous tail instead of legs. The child was about the size of a ballpoint pen and resembled a brownish earthworm with a Human head and torso. The next few eggs cracked in the same way as the camera flash caused them to curl up into a ring shape and let out a congealed screech.

"Should we name them now?" asked Shiv, looking at Yaj.

"I would wait for a few days," he said. "It can be hard to tell their sex when they're this small, but if you want to, go right ahead."

"Well," said Shiv, pointing at her slowly wriggling children. "There's Kanchana, Madhu, Mira, Durga, Harish, and…" She stopped once she noticed that one of the eggs hadn't hatched yet. "Honey?" said Shiv, freeing her tail and grabbing the unhatched egg. "Go take the kids to the kitchen and get the blended papaya."

"Of course, dear," said Yaj, taking the plastic bin out of the living room and into the spacious kitchen. He stood himself higher on his tail so that he could get to another plastic container filled with blended papaya. He grabbed the bin before slithering over to the knife stand, where he pulled a butter knife out. He spread small chunks of the blended papaya into the babies' bin before setting it on a marble countertop. The babies squirmed toward the reddish orange blob and began suckling on it like a nourishing blanket.

Later that evening, all the babies were placed in the same crib on the top level of the house. The remaining egg, however, sat alone well into the night as prime time sitcoms turned into talk shows. Yaj and Shiv sat on the couch all coiled up, but they weren't watching TV. Shiv teared up at the mere sight of the egg as Yaj patted her on the back and said, "I don't think it's going to hatch anytime soon."

"Why don't we wait!" said Shiv. "That was the last one I remember laying!"

"It would've hatched about now," said Yaj. "I think we should either eat it or leave it out in the field!"

Shiv thought long and hard about it. She wanted a full family of hatchlings, but she didn't want to part ways with her final remaining egg.

"I've thrown the shells in the garbage, now let's leave this one for the homeless," Yaj said. Shiv had begun to cry into her husband's body as he'd rub her back.

"Why must it be this way!" cried Shiv.

"I don't know, but that's what happens," said Yaj, letting go of Shiv. "Now, let's just put it out into the street"

"Okay," sniffled Shiv before she slithered her way over to the egg, and as if by magic, the egg began to crack just before she would've grabbed it with her fingers. The egg cracked much slower than the others, for each crack was followed by nearly several seconds of silence that felt like hours. The two were speechless as a hand eventually came out, soon followed by an arm before the rest of the body came out.

Expressions of amazement turned to horror when the baby came out with severe hatch defects. It had two extra arms in the form of vestigial nubs with fully formed fingers while his tail split in two a couple centimeters away from his cloaca, like stringy legs without hips. He didn't cry or squirm; he simply lay limp and stillhatched.

"This is horrible!"

"He certainly seems content otherwise," said Yaj.

"Much like Lord Shiva, ruler of Daksha," stated Shiv. "In fact, let's call him Dakshesh."

>━┥◀▶━◌━◀▶┝━<

Twenty-one years later, Dakshesh was the only one of his siblings to still live at home. He had his own room on the first level as his arm crutch laid against his bed while his dual green tails spread out and twist over each other like unsightly corkscrews. His lower two arms remain partly formed and not functional, as they constantly hugged his midsection. He spent his days playing video games and watching TV since his deformity kept him from working a regular job.

He rarely ever saw his father since Yaj was busy and preoccupied in Tamil Nadu legislature as well as federal parliament. On this day, Dakshesh sat in front of his bed watching a movie on a VCD changer when there was a knock on the bedroom door.

"Come in!" said Dakshesh before his mother opened the door.

"So, Dakshesh, I was just wondering what you wanted for lunch."

"I don't know," said Dakshesh, pausing the movie and turning around to look at his mother. "Maybe some curry or chow mein."

"What's wrong?" asked Shiv. "You seem down."

"I was just thinking," stated Dakshesh. "The Gods are there to mediate the lives of mortals, right?"

"Yes, they give us magic and blessings all the time," said Shiv. "That's why we keep Ganesha idols."

"So if that's the case, why did they make it so that I can barely move without a crutch!" argued Dakshesh.

"Well, it's so they can test us for reincarnation," said Shiv.

"Doesn't it seem a little cruel though?" stated Dakshesh cynically. "They make us only to have us suffer horribly with little control of our own lives!"

"Well, now we have control more than ever," explained Shiv.

"Yet no mortal could ever experience Godhood in the Hindu pantheon," said Dakshesh.

"Well, that's not our place to be," said Shiv.

"Like how it's not Dad's place to run for Prime Minister!" exclaimed Dakshesh. "Why don't we still have a monarchy if people were meant to be in these neat little boxes!"

"But that's different," said Shiv.

"How though!" said Dakshesh. "One concerns a country while the other concerns supernature. No amount of mantras, yogas, or medicine have made my condition any better! I swear these Gods just want to see us suffer!"

"Now I wouldn't say that," said Shiv.

"Mom!" exclaimed Dakshesh. "Look around. There're homeless people rummaging through the dumpsters, children dying before the age of five, and to top it off, the poor remain poor while we lap it up with our cars and our warm water!"

Shiv was speechless as Dakshesh turned off the TV and the VCD changer before he grabbed his phone and his wallet.

"If you can please make me something, I'd like to go out of town!"

"But Dakshesh, I—"

"You don't have to worry," he interrupted. "I know how to care for myself. I mean, it's not like I'm retarded or anything!"

After lunch, Dakshesh walked on his constantly swaying tails, using his arm crutch for balance. He looked down at his phone with his free hand for the nearest Buddhist sanghas, as he had been planning for the past several years. The only worship places that were in the town of Dharmapuri were Hindu temples, and Dakshesh lacked a car of his own. Despite his crippled nature, he was able to get to the train station.

He tried to coil up as best he could as he was sandwiched between a Human and a Vanara as he waited by the ticket booth. It was a good several minutes of enduring stares and curious gazes from onlookers before he got up to the ticket booth.

"I would like a one-way ticket to Arani, please," said Dakshesh with a smile.

"That will be 200 rupees," said the ticket master before Dakshesh reached into his shirt pocket and pulled out an orange

200-rupee note, putting it beneath the barrier and out the other side. The ticket master took the bill and put it in the register before passing the paper ticket back under the barrier. "Have a nice day" he said.

"You too!" replied Dakshesh before sitting on the bench and looking down at his tails. *I hope this works...* he thought as a diesel locomotive pulled into the station with a long line of coaches.

Once the train had stopped, people had walked out of the couches and clambered down their tops via ladders mounted to the coach's sides. Some Vanaras climbed up as their brown furred tails swayed out of their paints and freely flowing for balance. Dakshesh, however, got into the coach where a conductor punched his ticket, and he sat down in a bench with a table attatched to it so that his tails could fit beneath the table.

The train started going, and Dakshesh soon got out his phone as well as some earbuds. He untangled them and plugged them into the phone, and the earbuds were put in the ears. He watched a Let's play in the meantime, but the video got interrupted by an ad midway through, and it was an ad he was all too familiar with. It showed still images of poor people with no shoes and farmers laboring their fields as sad piano music played in the background. "India is not holy, and it is not perfect," read some on-screen Tamil text.

The ad, though currently skippable, played audio from the current Prime Minister's speeches with Tamil subtitles appearing at the bottom of the screen, for the commercial was otherwise in Hindi.

"To propel India into the new age," said Prime Minister Modi in Hindi, "I will stop the printing of notes that are 1,000 rupees or greater. It will bolster our IT and make us a true economic force in the world!" The audio was juxtaposed over videos of protesters holding signs up in an urban street and chanting.

"Does Modi truly know the people?" said a voice as pictures of market stalls in small towns came up next. "It is often said that those with power become detached from the citizen." The images faded out to a series of videos of Yaj speaking at various venues as well as addressing supporters face-to-face at a rally as the piano music became more upbeat. "The country doesn't need a great leap forward; the people need freedom of choice for the country."

The last few seconds show a grey haired Yaj in a suit and tie, looking at the camera as he said with a fanged smile: "I'm a firm believer in the free market and secular institutions based in the Krishna-given values of compassion for one's fellow man. A vote for me is a vote for India, I am Yaj Sivadi, and I approve this message."

Dakshesh teared upon seeing the ad, pausing it on his father's face.

"I'll do it for you, Father," he said as his voice broke up and patted the top of the screen. "I'll do it for you." Dakshesh put his phone into sleep mode and sniffled as he recalled seeing his father on TV and how amazing it was to see him in person as some words that Yaj told him during one of these rare times rang in his head: "You are who you are, extra tail or not. You will always be my son."

Later, the train stopped at Arani, and Dakshesh got off, careful to maneuver his tails so that they wouldn't be stepped on as he slowly and sadly walked from the train station through the middle of town toward the Arani Buddhist temple. There was a pile of shoes at the big archway into the temple complex as the air was dead silent. There was a Garuda in a long orange robe with his head shaven of any feathers and his reddish-grey scales accompanied by the white, green and yellow wing & body feathers gave him a rather dinosaur-like complexion.

He stood before the main entryway into the sangha itself, a humble building with traditional architectural elements along with elaborate statues of stoic Buddhas and guardian spirits. The Guru bowed humbly at Dakshesh.

"Good evening," said the Guru.

"Good evening to you, too," said Dakshesh, bowing in return. "I'm here for spiritual practice."

"You've come to the right place," smiled the Guru, noticing Dakshesh's arm crutch. "As you may be aware, the soul is made up of two components. The inself and the outself." He motioned to his chest tapping it a couple of times while Dakshesh nodded in understanding.

"The inself concerns your soul and how it comprises your personality as well as your inner dialog," explained the Guru. "But, the outself is your visual appearance, like your hair and style of clothing. But as it's so often the case, there is a disconnect between how you present yourself and how you truly are. The purpose of this meditation is to look into yourself and into your very soul, so that your true colors can show in the outself, so you can lead an honest life and so you can be true to yourself."

The Guru turned around and opened the door to the Sangha where a stone Buddha idol stood in a central shrine area with a couple believers bowing at the idol. Everyone walked into the sangha as the Guru said, "Now, choose any cushion you might like."

Dakshesh laid his arm crutch before his cushion before he coiled his tails together in a semi lotus position.

The door closed as the only light in the room came from the incense that burned at the altar. Dakshesh closed his eyes as the Guru sat down and struck a cylindrical bell, which made a ringing noise that slowly faded into silence, launching every sangha member into a state of peaceful meditation.

As he meditated, he felt his body sensation tingle and wane until he only felt his own inself. He soon felt an electric surge of otherworldly power as an image of spiral galaxies and spinning, eight-spoked wheels bending & warping came into his mind. A yellow-colored aura clouded his imagination as his outself began to transform, for his secondary arms began to grow until they were the size of his normal arms.

His tails merged into one as two more arms formed as his torso became taller and stronger. His aura was soon filled with incredible magic power that could be felt by everyone who was meditating in that room. Dakshesh's inself could perceive bodies of different shapes and sexes as well as the scenery surrounding the temple complex. His aura soon rivaled that of the Guru as cars and people appeared to be stepping in delayed segments like a constant reel of film being played at slow motion.

He had left his outself as it had coiled up as his spiritual essence teleported the sangha out of Arani and onto his mother's ranch in Dharmapuri. Dakshesh sweated as the Guru was amazed by all that was happening. Dakshesh soon conjured all sorts of colorful flowers into the sky before he gave his shirt four extra armholes. He was knocked out of meditation by another striking of the bell.

His inself was called back up as the bell was struck before it became fainter and fainter. Dakshesh was on the verge of blacking out, as he had completely exhausted the outself to pull off all those feats. Dakshesh's vision was snowy and blurry as he turned around and grabbed his arm crutch with his lowest left arm as he uncoiled himself. He still supported himself with his crutch, but only to ensure that he didn't pass out. As the Guru opened up the door, his jaw dropped when he found that tropical flowers had been falling from the sky onto a large countryside area.

Dakshesh smiled out of bliss as everything seemed like a blurry fever dream as his mother slithered out as roses, irises, and daisies pelted her and her tail as she noticed a strange sight. Dakshesh grabbed a lavender bud by the stem with his middle left hand. She was amazed to see a stronger, healthier Dakshesh with a Guru standing behind him.

"What is the meaning of this?" she asked in bewilderment, as all Dakshesh could do is moan and smile contentedly as his blurry vision was barely refocusing.

"Do you know her?" asked the Guru.

"She's my mother, and I don't regret anything," he said weakly before doing a feint chuckle.

"You should be proud," said the Guru. "Your son has achieved upondasana, a meditation so intense that it alters reality!"

Everything that had happened was so quick and amazing that she broke down in tears at Dakshesh's now powerful tail.

Dakshesh patted her with his bottom right hand and wrapped his middle right arm around the Guru to piggyback his already strong aura to heal his own stamina.

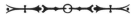

In the following days, the town of Dharmapuri had begun to praise Dakshesh as an avatar of the God Vishnu, much to the dismay of Dakshesh himself. He soon became a local celebrity because of his seemingly Godlike powers, even after they had to clean their cars, houses, and driveways of leftover flowers. Though Yaj didn't get to be the Prime Minister, he took that as an opportunity to live with his family as one unit, and they all lived happily sometimes after.

The End

11
CHARITY OF THE DEMONS

If you could walk the streets of the Romanian city of Cluj-Napoca, you'd see a string of open manholes as well as some street signs that read "Caution: Vampire Hazard" as a crude diagram of a fanged person emerging would appear beneath. It was an overcast night as a young Elven woman named Iuliana walked out of the bus and down some brick streets. People got on the bus as it announced, "Route 112, Clujana Station via Fabricii."

The street was otherwise relatively quiet save for some passing cars as the woman passed by that very street sign on her way home. She was browsing through Twitter and wasn't paying attention to her surroundings as an open manhole laid mere centimeters away from where she was walking. A deathly pale hand with sharp claws emerged from the manhole to grab her by the ankle.

She dropped her phone down onto the street as she tripped and fell onto the brick sidewalk. Her face became bruised and bloodied while her phone screen became cracked. Another hand came out to drag her across the sidewalk and into the sewer.

"Hey!" exclaimed Iuliana, grabbing her phone. "Get your disgusting hands off me!" She thrashed and thrashed against the arms as they kept dragging her across the sidewalk.

Almost before she knew it, Iuliana's whole body was pulled down into the manhole as she gripped the rim with all her might. She couldn't hold on anymore, and as her grip gave way, she was finally dragged down into the sewer as she let out a blood-curdling scream. The manhole had steel, ladder-like steps that were bolted into the concrete walls. One Vampire held her tightly as the other closed the manhole above them. The first one tied Iulianna up in chains as she took a few breaths. The two Vampires proceeded to carry her down the manhole's steps as Iuliana exclaimed, "What are you going to do me?"

She got no answer, as club music could be heard from further down in the manhole.

At the bottom of the ladder was a hot, misty room with plenty of electric lanterns illuminating the dark alcove. A lone boombox served as the source of the music, and used heroin needles littered the grey concrete floor. Pipes weaned around the halls and hallways as a periodic pulsing sound filled the room as well as the sounds of people flushing their toilets in surrounding apartments. She was amazed and disgusted by her surroundings as she exclaimed, "What's going on here! What do you people want with me?"

"You're going to help us," said one Vampire.

"You're going to give us a spot in society," explained the other.

"You monsters are probably going to tell me that just so you can eat me," she said as they escorted her through some hallways.

"Far from it," said the Vampire "You're gonna meet with White Blood."

"Oh shit," she muttered, remembering a newscast about someone with that code name. "I'm not gonna be a chip in your drug schemes."

But before the Vampires could object, they tossed her into a sizable brick chamber filled with shirts and blankets. Sat on top of the mound was a snowy-white man with red eyes, a rectangular face with a sharp nose, long yet rounded ears and black colored claws. He wore a black & white patterned hoodie, a button-down shirt, a silver cross necklace, and a crown comprised of cardboard, packaging tape & accents of powdery white cocaine.

"I know who you are, and I want nothing to do with you!" the Elf pouted.

"Foolish girl," he said, grinning with a fanged smile. "I don't want you for my enterprise."

"Well, why did you and your goons drag me down here!" she exclaimed.

"You see, across the road is for attention," he said, running his clawed pointer finger across his forearm. "Down the stream goes to the morgue." He proceeded to run his finger down toward his elbow.

"Wh-what is that supposed to mean?" she said frantically.

"It means that society doesn't want us to exist," he explained. "I didn't become White Blood by asking for handouts. These streets took me in and raised me when no one else wanted to. We carved these tunnels to look out for each other. These are my people, and I'm like their king."

"But do you really have to cause all this havoc!" she exclaimed. "People are scared to leave their house because of you!"

"People around here are very superstitious, as you're aware," remarked White Blood. "As far as people on the streets know, Demons like us are evil monsters causing their kids to get seizures or some shit! Truth is though: Folks like us fit right into God's plan. He created man and beast, the cow eats the plants, the humans eat the plants and the cow, and we eat the humans and the cow to keep them from being evil & overpopulating the planet. It's all part of the grand circle of life."

"Oh," she said, "and I'm sure Satan has something to do with this."

"This order is much older than him and has been with us for billions of years," he said. "But he's an Angel who merely disagreed with our Lord and Savior thousands of years back."

""You people belong in hell!" she exclaimed

"There's plenty of us down there, too. But why be in hell when you can make Earth better?" shrugged White Blood. "I've used my earnings to fund a new referendum for Parliament."

"That being?" asked Iuliana.

"Referendum V," he said. "It's to ensure that the police won't slay us on sight."

"Don't they want to keep people from turning into Vampires like yourself?" asked Iuliana with a raised eyebrow.

"I only put that curse on my venom when I want to," he said. "We are carnivorous, and we need meat in order to survive. Lychans are running the supermarkets, and we're down here in the sewers. No one would believe any of us if we campaigned for this to go through Bucharest."

"I feel so sorry for you," she said, "But knowing your straits now, I'd be more than willing to help."

"Great," smiled White Blood, getting out a small printout of a campaign poster. "Now, at your work or whatever, tape this to your shirt and get people on board with our cause by any means necessary."

"Don't worry, I'll make sure that you won't have to do that," she said. "Have a good evening."

"You too," replied White Blood.

In the following days, Iuliana started a new Facebook account called "YesonV" and littered it with various trivia about Vampires, from the toxicity of their venom to how they evolved from Homo Habilis along with Humans, Orks, Neanderthals and Elves.

"Vote Yes on V," she said to passersby as she stood outside of her university. "Vampires have feelings like you and me, so get them some sympathy to vote yes on V!"

People passed by ignoring Iuliana, as most just went about their business until a tall, dark green man with two sharp tusks walked by and Iuliana said, "Vampires need our sympathy, so vote yes on V."

"Do you honestly think that Vampires are Human?" he asked.

"You see, they evolved fro—"

"Yes or no?"

"We—"

"Yes or no?"

Iuliana rolled her eyes.

"No," she said begrudgingly. "Bu—"

"Well, they don't deserve Human rights then, do they?" he said before walking down to the end of the block.

"Vampire lives matter as much as everyone else's, and you know it!" she exclaimed, pointing at him.

She soon resumed to her post as a bus stopped nearby.

"Vote yes on Referendum V," she said to the leaving passengers.

"I'm not registered because the system is rigged in every election," said a fair-skinned man as he walked right past her.

"Your voice matters regardless of who stays in Parliament," remarked Iuliana

"What does Referendum V even do anyways?" asked another person who stopped in her tracks.

"Well," said Iulianna, "Transylvania Vampires live in our sewers in fear because they're being killed on sight once they surface. It seems unfair that Werewolves can live their lives peacefully, but Vampires can't. Prop V will give Vampires the same legal protections as you or me because every predator deserves a right to life."

"Interesting," she said. "I'll go check it out."

"If you want to learn more, go to Facebook and type in 'Yes on V' and learn some surprising facts about Vampkind."

The other lady soon walked into the campus as Iuliana zipped up her coat and walked into the campus and sat down in history class as if nothing happened. She sat down and got out her notebook as her teacher, Mr. Romanescu, got up in front of the podium.

"So, as always, before we go into today's lesson, what's happening in the world right now?" asked Mr. Romanescu.

"Muslim refugees were like stopped at our border," said a girl shyly.

"Right, Islam coming to our country," he said, stroking his chin. "Anything else?" asked the teacher, pointing to another raised hand. "Yes?"

"Vampires breaking into our Parliament," said the student

"Vampires need a voice, and they've been silenced like this since the Ottoman period," exclaimed Iuliana. "If we treated them more like people then they wouldn't be living in the sewers."

"Iuliana, I appreciate your enthusiasm, but we're talking about these bloodthirsty monsters," said the teacher.

"But they can't help it," she explained, unzipping her jacket, "which is why I've been campaigning for the past couple of weeks for Vampire rights in this country."

"You can be an activist, but can you keep the activism out of the class," he said. "You're causing a disruption"

"Sorry," replied Iuliana before she zipped her jacket back up and proceeded to take notes on the lecture. After class, she went on the bus in the afternoon back to the manhole she was first dragged down. Though noble as her intentions were, the next time she went down into the sewers, the tunnels were lined with carcasses as homeless dined on intestines and livers like a macabre version of Thanksgiving. Seeing this made her stomach turn as the heads of humans and Lychans hung on the wall like a trophy hunter's taxidermy. Her face lost all color as she walked into White Blood's chamber to find him absent.

"Hello?" she said. "White Blood?" she asked, wandering around the chamber. "I want to speak with you." There was no one there for a good several minutes as she sat on top of some blankets. Then she heard a hatch open up in the distance. White

Blood could be seen walking in, counting a large stack of Lei notes as he chuckled to himself.

"Ah, Iulianna, so good to see you," he said as he saw her.

"I want to tell you that people are fairly receptive to the proposition, you can be out of here."

"It's too late for me," he said. "If I was up they're, they'd put me in prison anyways on drug charges and 'murder.'"

"I'm sure they could rehabilitate you," she said, "even to make you Human again."

"I'm the guardian of the homeless!" he exclaimed "They'd be freezing their asses off on the streets if it weren't for me. I make their life bearable and give them a safe shelter."

"I would think it's degrading to be living down here!" she exclaimed. "How can you exploit people like that by imprisoning them like this!"

White Blood soon walked toward Iuliana as he drew his fangs out.

"You know too much. You'll blow the cover on my enterprise," he said. "They'd get evicted out of here the moment I'm arrested, and everyone who lives here will be forced into the concentration camps they call shelters!" He soon bit into the tender part of her neck, sinking his acidic venom into her bloodstream. The color faded from her face as her body went limp, and she passed out onto a pile of jackets.

White Blood dragged her into the main mess hall, where her remains were butchered and eaten. No one ever saw or heard from Iuliana since, and they all lived tragically ever after.

The End

12
FERAL MASTERMIND

It was a sweltering 35-degree summer day at the Alice Springs International Airport in the Australian outback, a 33-year-old man named Frank walked through the skybridge into the terminal. He had a modest patterned gray cloth bag on his shoulder and could be seen looking around the sleek airport terminal for signs to the baggage claim.

Here at last, he thought, working his way toward the escalator. *Can't wait to see Jim again.* Frank got his phone out of his pocket and proceeded to take it off airplane mode while stepping onto the escalator. His phone lit up with many messages and notifications with persistent tones accompanying each one. Frank was heavily tempted to put his phone back into his pocket until a news notification made his eyes wide with fear and concern.

"Thirty found dead in Alice Springs" read the news notification as Frank proceeded to tap on it before it redirected him to an article on the phone's built-in news app. "Over the past week, 30 have been killed around the Alice Springs area," read the article. "Witnesses report the sighting of swiftly disappearing animals around the time of the killings. Police suspect far-right incels may be behind this most recent bout of magical terrorism."

He winced upon reading it before he put his phone back in his pocket and slowly walked toward the baggage claim, looking for the luggage carousel belonging to his flight. Locals, meanwhile, crowded around the airport windows, gazing upon a flock of wood swallows perched on a sidewalk railing. A feared murmur was heard among the crowd of locals all the while Frank worked his way to the baggage claim, shaking his head and wincing at the thought of being killed.

"Not going over there," mumbled Frank before sitting on the bench by the baggage claim for his flight. Once Fred sat down, he got his phone out, unlocked it, and played a game to pass the time as a few kids ran around screaming in exhilaration after being cooped up in an airplane for so long. He kicked his feet up against the metal siding of the baggage claim and played until an electric buzzing noise was heard.

The metal blades of its conveyer began moving, and people walked towards it awaiting their suitcases. Soon enough, their luggage would come from a conveyer belt out the top of the carousel before falling on the carousel blades with a large *thunk!* People grabbed their luggage as Frank glanced up from his phone to look for his bag before he went back to the phone and continued playing.

Suddenly, Frank spotted people leaving the baggage claim out the corner of his eye. He put his phone to sleep and swiftly put it in his pocket and looked towards the people.

"Wait, what's going on?" he asked turning his head.

"S-spider!" exclaimed a young woman, pointing at a black widow on Frank's suitcase.

"Oh!" exclaimed Frank before he yanked his suitcase out of the baggage claim, carefully putting it on the ground. Next, he proceeded to grab a plastic cup as well as a napkin from out of his bag. He carefully held the napkin down toward the spider and readied the cup to trap it.

The spider crawled onto the napkin, but just as Frank forced the plastic cup onto the napkin, it leapt onto his left arm and bit him. Frank yelped in pain and tried to swat the spider before it started digging into his flesh. Yellow fatty tissue oozed out of the wound and down his arm as deep, red blood gushed out, streaking down his wrist and dripping on the floor. The spider burrowed below the skin, eviscerating fat and muscle with its mandibles until it grabbed onto a blood vessel and bit it. Frank, meanwhile, fell to the floor with a thud, his body laying limp and growing more pale by the second. The blood-soaked spider climbed out of the wound while people screamed and ran away upon seeing such a grotesque sight. Once the witnesses had run away to call the police, the spider vanished into thin air. All that remained was a grotesque, bloodied open wound on a corpse as white as porcelain.

Little over 16 kilometers away at the Pine Gap Military Base, a lone American Military Police officer by the name of Jim patrolled the grounds with an assault rifle in hand and a fearful gaze on his face. He took several stoic steps in the perimeter, but his eyes were perched wide open, for a bizarre enemy had left hundreds at the base dead with little sign of struggle.

A mortician and a sorry Army surgeon could be seen wearing latex gloves carefully dragging a body wearing the uniform of an Australian private into a body bag.

"Halt" said Jim while drawing his gun. "Who goes there!"

"Whoah, mate!" exclaimed the mortician, holding his hands up with the surgeon soon following. "It's me—Dan."

"Oh," said Jim, "I'm so sorry. In a time like this, you never know what's going on."

"I get it" replied Dan before zipping up the body bag. "Now let's go to the morgue. The last of us are taking shelter there!"

Jim nodded and proceeded to follow them towards a modest shack at the corner of the perimeter. They went down a flight of stairs that would end in a large steel door as Jim opened the door, revealing a white sterile room with metallic accenting, an autopsy table, and several mortuary chambers with large steel drawers.

The Doctor and the mortician would haul the body bag into an open mortuary chamber as the refrigeration brought relief from the scorching heat. There were now six living people in the morgue, each with feared looks written across their faces. Their uniforms were tattered and torn as they shivered in their grim shelter.

"Jim?" said a man in the highly decorated uniform of a Provost Marshal. "You're alive!"

"Yes, sir," said Jim solemnly. "But it was absolute hell up there. Dingos burrowing out of the ground, snakes on the fences, and falcons swarming around covert operatives."

The Marshal soon turned towards Dan and asked, "How many casualties?"

"I've recorded 802 deaths," said Dan, carefully sliding the body out of its bag, toes first. "We're the last ones alive, and I'm the only Australian here on the whole base."

"That does raise an interesting point," said the Doctor. "When the animals first came, they targeted only Australian personal and then us Americans were next, and I suspect they have the same mana signature as all the others."

"Certainly a unique one," remarked Dan, throwing the body bag in the biowaste disposal area. "It reeks of divine essence, like a deity, but they are so similar to one another that all these different animals could well be all the same person." Dan looked over at the database on his phone and back to the soldier's nametag. Dan wrote his name, date of birth, rank, and time of death, but just as he was going to put on the victim's toe tag, the body turned transparent and faded into thin air.

The two jumped at the sight.

"Did you guys see that?" asked Dan, looking around the room bug-eyed.

"I did," said the Doctor, closing his eyes and working yellow-colored magic around his fingers before uttering a Greek incantation under his breath and letting it zip around the vacant chamber for a few seconds. He soon opened his eyes and said, "Whatever spirit made them disappear must be the same one that's been killing all those people."

"But why here?" asked Jim. "We're practically built for intelligence gathering with all these satellites on the base"

"Maybe it's an act of intimidation," conjected Marshal Harris, "like a cocky serial killer. It wants us to be afraid, so it can facilitate whatever its planning."

"But, sir," said Jim, "what would some otherworldly being even have to gain from offing us mortals?"

"I don't know," replied the Marshal as the wall phone began to ring. "But what I do know is that whatever this God is, it's compromising national security for Australia and the United States alike."

One of the few remaining soldiers picked up and answered the phone.

"You've reached the Pine Gap joint defense base, Private Cortez speaking," answered the soldier before standing in silence as the person on the other end spoke. "Warrant Officer Alfredson?" he asked. "Hold on. I'll get him." The soldier soon held the handle of the phone away from himself. "Jim," he said. "It's for you."

Jim proceeded to walk over to the phone before he grabbed the handle and held it to the side of his face.

"Hello?" he answered.

"I'm Constable Pengarte of the Northern Territory police force," said the voice, "and I have something important to tell you."

"Oh?" inquired Jim.

"I'm sorry to tell you this, but your brother Frank has been murdered," said the constable solemnly. "His body was found at the airport before it vanished."

"Oh," sighed Jim, rubbing his face, taking a moment to grieve. "I understand."

"We'll do everything we can," said the constable sadly.

"I know," said Jim. "Same thing happened at the Army morgue."

"Streuth," said the constable breathlessly. "Sounds like we need to collaborate our efforts to solve the case, if it's alright with your superior."

"I would think so," said Jim. "He's the only one left to run the base, and even he says it compromises security, because it's killed pretty much all the personnel."

"Well, it sounds like we ought to crack the case before it goes after more civilians," said the constable "I'll be there in a half hour."

"Park outside by the main gate," instructed Jim. "This is an international satellite base where security is paramount, even during crisis."

"Right," said the constable with a tone of understanding. "Goodbye officer."

"Bye," replied the officer, hanging up before turning towards the Marshal.

"Who was it?" asked the Marshal

"It was the police, sir," explained Jim. "They want to collaborate with us on a joint operation."

"Whatever for?" asked the Marshal "These things are well beyond their purview."

"This…thing has been offing civilians for a while now, sir," said Jim. "One of them was my brother who came to visit me, and I have to do something."

"I understand your grief, but don't let it get to you," said the Marshal. "You could be next!"

"Even if I am, sir," said Jim, "I'd die defending a longstanding American ally."

"Not like we can defend ourselves at this point," said Dan.

"I'm the only Australian on base, but I'm a mortician, not a soldier, and besides, I don't even have combat training."

"Looks like we'll have to muster more troops," said the Marshal, stroking his chin. "And if you end up getting killed by that thing, there goes any chance of security."

"With God on my side, I can make the doors impenetrable," suggested the surgeon.

"I suppose I could call the Australian bases," said the Marshal. "Their Wizards could teleport more troops here."

"And I'll wait for the constable to come by," said Jim. "I can gather intel, and I can defend myself, sir."

"Good thinking," said the Marshal. "The entire country is counting on you, Jim, don't mess this up."

"I won't, sir," said Jim, walking out of the morgue, shutting the door behind him.

⊱ ⊰ ⊙ ⊱ ⊰

A half hour later, a lone police cruiser parked outside the perimeter of the base while Jim stood waiting in a deserted guard post by the large imposing metal gate with a bottle of water in hand. Jim spotted the car and proceeded to walk out of the guard post before carefully locking it. He walked over to the lefthand side of the car and briefly eyeballed the driver, for he was a bizarre sight.

The constable was a reddish-tan, furred kangaroo with a long face and a blue uniform with a black vest and matching navy-blue hat that concealed his ears. Jim quietly got in the car and shut the door.

"Uhh," he said, putting on his seat belt and trying to avert his gaze.

"You weren't expecting me to be a Kangaroo?" asked Constable Pengarte.

"Well," said Jim as the constable turned back towards the desert road. "I mean like a lizard or a dingo sure, but a kangaroo is just... odd, don't take it the wrong way though"

"Ah, no worries," said Constable Pengarte before he proceeded to drive down the road. "I get that a lot, name's Penangke."

"Well, hello," said the officer. "I'm Jim, n-nice to meet you."

"Good to see you, too, Jim," said Penangke. "You seem pretty scared for an American soldier."

"Well, I don't want to be rude," said Jim. "But it's not every day you work with a talking animal!"

"Can't decide how I was born," said Penangke. "As a forensic Shaman, I keep my shape the way I keep my magic powers."

"Cool," said Jim, as his mind was filled with curiosity of Aboriginal culture as a voice came over the walkie talkie.

"We've got another 6-1-2 at Traeger Park, over."

"Constable Pengarte coming in," radioed Penangke. "I'll be there to investigate, over and out."

The park was completely deserted and roped off with caution tape by the time they got there. There were no shortages of places to park as people took shelter in nearby homes and hotels leaving the city dead silent and desolate. Penangke would park the car by the curb near the park where he unbuckled his seat belt and opened the door.

Jim proceeded to open the door before walking towards the sidewalk where Penangke hopped out before locking the cruiser. The two walked towards a large area of the park sectioned off by caution tape as a few of the constables could be seen overlooking the body of a middle-aged woman. The body was riddled with bitemarks and blood spatter, but most mysteriously was the lack of footprints on the ground.

"Little out of your jurisdiction, aren't we?" pouted one of the constables as Jim stepped under the caution tape and Penangke bounded over it.

"I'd rather not be," explained Jim, trying to swallow his grief, "but it struck at the Pine Gap base, and whatever's going on could threaten national security both for my country as well as yours!"

The constables nodded in understanding as Penangke leapt towards the body and joined his colleagues.

"So, I assume this is another supernatural ambush," said Penangke grimly.

"Looks like it," said a constable. "Now, Shaman, would you mind working your magic to lead us to a suspect?"

"That's no problem," said Penangke as he proceeded to draw white-colored magic out of his left hand and look down at the bitemark. "Seems consistent for a dingo bite. Now to get some answers…" He cast deep purple colored magic as he chanted in his native Arrernte. "Return your soul from the Dreaming, so life can flow through flesh and bone."

The magic began to flow into the body's nose as a cracking sound emanated from her joints, and she opened her eyes, dazed and confused.

"Uh, where am I?" she asked, trying to rub her temple.

"You're out in the park," said Penangke. "Something murdered you. Now, would you mind telling us what you saw once you died?"

"I-it was weird," said the lady as Penangke helped her up. "Th-there were ancestors going back to the middle ages, but they were put under mind control by this-this lizardman and a snake that was all rainbow-colored."

"Interesting," said Penangke, stroking his maw. "Did you happen to get their names?"

"Y-yeah," said the lady "Their names we—" She was interrupted by her body swiftly dissolving into white ash that piled up on the ground as an unusual, smooth laughing call of a bird was heard from the trees. All the constables looked up at the bird. It was stout with long teal and blue feathers.

"A kookaburra?" asked one of the constables in bewilderment.

"Uh oh," said Penangke before drawing his gun. "Alright, wings where I can see them!"

"Whoa, what are you guys doing!" exclaimed Jim. "It's just one bird!"

"Kookaburras prefer more coastal areas!" explained Penangke while the bird flew down from the tree and began to hover in midair while slowing the flap of her wings. Sandy-brown-colored magic emanated from its wings, creating an enormous gust of wind that ripped streetlights from their foundation and personnel off their feet, launching them towards an abandoned playground.

"Well," said the kookaburra menacingly. "Haven't we been colonized!"

Jim and the constables soon got up and began shooting at the kookaburra, who began flying in circles, making her impossible to hit. In response, she made a deep-pink-colored energy field and proceeded to dart towards an Elven constable at supersonic speed, creating a small sonic boom behind her.

Before they knew it, the bird was covered in blood while the constable screamed in pain.

"Constable Presson!" exclaimed another constable, turning over to him as he fell in the sand before he frantically grabbed his walkie talkie and said: "constable down, there is a 1-13, request backup!"

Penangke soon bounded after the bird as Jim took cover behind the tree. The bird swerved and darted around the park, billowing sparks from her feathers. Penangke would soon counter it with a water spell as she closed her wings and maneuvered below Penangke, barely grazing the bottom of his tail before she slid through the grass and Jim fired a couple rounds into the body of the bird.

She tried letting out a loud pained call, but it was little use. Penangke turned around and began chanting, "Great ancestor spirit, strip this dreamtime miscreant of any divine power." Penangke began to brace himself as yellow energy struck the bird with an electric shock until it turned into a forcefield to contain her.

"Aren't you a little young to be doing this?" asked the kookaburra as koalas began to materialize out of the trees.

"None of your business," retorted Penangke. "This isn't even my fir—" He was soon interrupted by a sudden weight on his back as a koala fell from the tree and bit him.

"Drop bears!" exclaimed one of the constables while the the kookaburra freed herself from the newly dispelled barrier. "Let's get out of here!"

Penangke wiped away the bear before it could do real damage as he rapidly hopped away from the grove, riddled with fear. Jim, meanwhile, practically jumped before he looked up the gum tree's bark to see a dark grey bear falling from one of the branches. He rolled out of the way as the small bear slammed headfirst into the ground. A small sonic boom sounded, and the kookaburra flew out of town and into the desert.

The party soon ran out of the trees while the drop bears on the ground fired magic beams from their eyes, and others clawed their uniforms to shreds. Backup swiftly arrived with sirens blaring as the grounds had turned into something of a spiritual warzone. Penangke landed on the hood of his patrol car, creating a massive dent in its middle. He helplessly flailed his legs, for the gang of predators brought him back to a feral childhood in the desert while a sea of gunfire emanated from the park.

"Dude!" exclaimed Jim before jogging around the front of the car. "What's going on, and why are you laying around on your own damn car!"

"They're after me!" exclaimed Penangke. "They hate civilization, and they're gonna eat me... Gotta go!"

"Yeah, let's go!" said Jim, trying to open the driver's side door. "I'll drive. You're too hysterical to go anywhere, so can you please unlock the car!"

"No!" exclaimed Penangke as a troop of kangaroos materialized onto the road. "I'll leap to safety. C'mon, guys, let's get the fuck out of here!"

"You don't have to keep running—er, hopping!" exclaimed Jim as the kangaroos began to block the front bumper. "You're more than a mere animal. You can fight back against this now!"

"No, Human!" exclaimed Penangke. "I don't fight; I run. Isn't that right, guys!"

The kangaroos leapt onto the hood and stood on Penangke, pinning him down as constables ran to their patrol cars. "How could you do this, my own troop!"

"No," said Jim before cocking his gun. "It's likely a trick by the entity; the only troop you belong to is the troupe of cops. You're a constable, not an animal!"

"You know what," said Penangke. "You're right! Me feral kind would never wish this on me!" He proceeded to draw his own gun and shot at two of the assailants, kicked another off the hood of the car, and Jim fired two rounds in the last one's back. He ran to the passenger side while the kangaroo corpses vanished into thin air.

Penangke soon proceeded to roll himself off the hood and hopped towards the driver's side, where he got in and proceeded to buckle his seatbelt.

"Awaiting spiritual direction on the 5-1-6, over," radioed a fellow constable.

"Copy that," replied Penangke before putting the walkie talkie back on his belt, and chanting in Arrernte, he was given a vivid vision of two Gods standing outside of town with Earth military personal nearby. "The culprits are out in the outback. I'm enroute to the suspect."

"Copy that," replied the constable before Penangke returned it to his belt, started his cruiser and swiftly drove away while activating his siren. The convoy of cops would soon race through the street swerving around corners and between lanes. "So where in the desert might this guy be?" asked Jim.

"He should be just south of here," replied Penangke before he tapped the car's two-way radio with his claw. "I can sense his aura getting stronger, I'm enroute to the source." He tapped it again, ending the transmission.

"Copy that," replied a constable. "We're following you enroute to the suspect."

Just outside of the desert stood two Arrernte Gods, one of them was a giant snake with a rainbow scale pattern named Julunggul; the other was a sandy yellow lizard man named Mangar Kunjer Kunja, holding a petrified tree branch in hand.

"I can't keep distracting the mortals for much longer," complained Julunggul. "They're gonna catch onto us at some point."

"Why do you worry so much, hun?" asked Mangar, patting Julunggul's colorful abdomen "We're Deities, they can't do anything to stop us even if they tried. Australia will always be for Australians, not Britains."

"I'm sorry to tell you, but we have a welcoming committee," said Julunggul as she stretched herself straight up and pointed the end of her tail towards a cavalcade of soldiers, armored vehicles, and rocket launchers moving towards them.

"I'll deal with them," said Mangar with a sinister grin plastered across his maw. "Come from the dreaming to extinguish the invaders!" he chanted as the branch glowed blue and fired magic at the sand, creating a field of light more intense than the sun. The troops held their hands in front of their faces as the tanks stopped advancing until the light cleared away to reveal flanks of 20,000 dingoes with the deafening sound of snarling piercing the air. A tank barrel was pointed down at the dingoes, and a mortar was fired as the swarm of wild dogs promptly overtook the soldiers.

Despite the machine gun fire and magic, the bedlam of sheer numbers persisted over the battlefield. Some dogs would be seen jumping and biting at the troops. Some were able to shake them while others were soon mauled and disemboweled.

Tanks mowed down the dingoes' bodies with no effort as Julunggul soon flew over the chaotic battlefield and fired differently colored rays at the tanks, dissolving them into nothing as the tank operators were rapidly overtaken by the swarm of dingoes.

All seemed hopeless as Mangar just stood and watched the carnage as a fleet of cop cars could be seen in the distance.

"You are under arrest for first degree murder, anything you say and do can and will be used against you in a court of law!" exclaimed Penangke through the cruiser's loudspeaker in Arrernte. "And as an Arrernte Elder, you are exceeding your own damn code."

Mangar smirked at this and blasted an invisible radiation spell at the cruisers before Penangke radioed to his fellow constables. "There's a ball of radioactive goo headed towards us at twelve o clock, over!"

"Copy that," replied one of the others as they swerved beyond the dirt road path only to have most of the flank blasted with radioactive energy, toasting the cars into twisted melting piles of metal and flames. There were two cruisers left as Mangar summoned a flock of eagles and a kangarooman spirit to peck and claw the remaining cruisers to pieces.

"You are a disgrace to your band!" complained the spirit, sabotaging the car's engine and steering system. Penangke soon lost control and swerved into the outback sand, kicking up an enormous cloud of dust in the process. Jim ran out of the car, coughing up dust as he made out the imposing silhouette of the God.

Once the dust settled, Mangar was plainly visible as Julungul slithered through the air behind his back.

"You've killed every damn person in town, destroyed my comrades, and killed my own brother, so why don't you eat lead, dragon breath!" he exclaimed and fired his machine gun at Mangar. The bullets tore through his flesh, but just as quickly as he was shot, he was healed and even pouted to intimidate the mortals.

He looked down at his gun dumbfounded, thinking, *This cartridge is enchanted, how is this not working?*

"Who even cares about a meager town of 26,000?" mused Mangar. "The world's eyes are on the millions of hectares ablaze, and in order to get rid of the pest, I need to smoke you European vermin out!"

"Your Holiness!" exclaimed Penangke indignantly, bounding towards him while a lone American tank crept towards the Gods "They gave me the opportunity to do good in the world in ways I couldn't have imagined."

"You really think your magic is to be admired, boy?" asked Mangar. "You're only six, and you're already doing chants. These spells are too dangerous for such a young and feral mind!"

"No, I am older if you count both lifetimes," complained Penangke. "I've guarded the sacred sites, so what if it's not tradition. I've made a good life for myself, and I don't see the problem."

"You are disobeying your Creator and paramount Life Carver!" said the spirit. "You're a disgrace to the Pengarte clan, in the face of your Creator. As your ancestral spirit, you ought to be ashamed!"

"Ashamed of what?" asked Penangke as the tank fired its mortar. "That I'm not living in a tent like some kind of caveman?!"

"I should've never let them rebirth you," said Julunggul, dispelling the shell into seemingly thin air. "I don't see any cousins here, nor do I see you sharing water with neighboring communities. You've completely abandoned the Arrernte covenant."

"Not if I have anything to say about that!" exclaimed Dr. Urich.

"Dr. Urich?" asked Jim. "What in the world are you doing here, and why are you speaking the Aboriginal language?"

"It'll all make sense to you someday," he replied, as he, the Gods, and the spirits all vanished in the blink of an eye without a trace.

"What the hell happened?" asked Jim.

"In the magic business, nothing makes sense," retorted Penangke. "Even when you think you know, you don't. And that was a right heroic thing you did, even if you didn't make a dent, you still stood your ground."

"Thanks," said Jim. "If only Frank was alive to see it."

"Well, what if I said I can bring him back?" said Penangke.

"What, like resurrect him?" asked Jim.

"His body doesn't exist anymore, and his soul has moved on," explained Penangke. "Julunggul dissolved them all, but there is a way I could still resurrect him."

"What do you mean?" asked Jim

"Induced reincarnation," explained Penangke. "In the traditional covenant of my people, the Arrernte, souls flow between different parts of nature be it man or beast. I used to be an Elf in the previous lifetime, and I worked as a constable all the way down in Melbourne. After being given the opportunity to leave the northern territories in favor of the hustle and bustle of the big city."

I dealt in apprehending suspects, like murderers and rapists, all usual if not jarring business. I've had colleagues die until that point, so I wasn't too surprised to end up in the Dreaming as I'd been involved in a gang shootout. I remained there for well over two weeks until my folks paid for an elder to resurrect me through a process called induced reincarnation. I was reborn as a kangaroo as part of the dreaming cycle, and from then on, I dedicated my life to magic as a way to give back to those that gave me a second chance at life.

"Well, that sounds great," said Jim. "Frank just came here to visit and now he'll get his wish."

"Well, at a cost," said Penangke.

"Oh?" inquired Jim.

"The brain is like a hard drive, it controls many functions, but the memory that's on it gets wiped away once it goes kaput," explained Penangke. "Certain things may well be backed up in the soul, but whatever's left will leave the new body a clean slate."

"Meaning?" asked Jim.

"Meaning that there's a good chance that Frank could lose any sense of self or any memory of his Human life," replied Penangke. "To put it simply: You just may never see Frank again."

"Woah," said Jim as he thought about the offer while he hung his head in sadness, feelings of grief hitting him like a ton of bricks. "Yes," he said, rubbing his hands in his face. "Reincarnate him or whatever, just so I can see Frank again."

"That'll be $200," said Penangke, holding his hand out as Jim gave him a long glare. "Hey, wands and mana don't grow on trees."

"I guess not," replied Jim. "I'll pay you after everything is said and done with the base, alright?" He brought his hand out, and Penangke nodded, saying, "Alright, that sounds like a deal." He brought his hand out and shook Jim's hand.

A few weeks later, Penangke could be seen by a modest home on the outskirts of town wearing a T-shirt as his tail bowed out from a small hole in the back of his jeans. Jim soon parked his car in front of the home before he turned it off and walked out in his dress uniform.

"Good to see you, mate," smiled Penangke. "If you don't mind me asking, what's with the uniform?"

"I just came back from a press conference," explained Jim. "The Marshal just promoted me to Chief Warrant Officer for maintaining order during a time of crisis."

"That's great," said Penangke.

"Yeah, I know, right?" said Jim before looking around. "So this is the dog breeder's, huh?"

"Yes, it is. I routed the his soul here," clarified Penangke.

"Oh," said Jim, "I just wasn't expecting it to be soo…shabby."

"Hey, I know the lady who runs this. She's a real beauty," said Penangke, hopping in while Jim followed. There was an older woman standing in the hallway, saying, "Hey Penangke, thanks for saving the town."

"Hey, I was just doing my job," replied Penangke. "But anyways, do you have a dog named Frank?"

"Yes, we do," replied the lady. "As a matter of fact, he's in the newest litter of puppies."

"That's great," said Jim. "Can I see him?"

"Of course," said the lady, walking into the backyard. "Right this way."

In the back were dogs of various breeds and ages walking about the backyard as a stack of kennels lay in front of the rear fence. She looked over the puppies carefully to find Frank among the newborn white and brown basset hounds. She looked down at the different collars and tags until she came across one of the larger puppies named Frank.

"There you are, little guy," she said, picking him up and holding him by the arm.

"Wow," he said. "He's actually kinda cute."

"And I'm sure he's gonna be a brother to you," she said.

"Wait," replied Jim. "How did you...?"

"Penangke told me," explained the breeder.

"Right," said Penangke. "Should we go inside and conduct business?"

"Of course," replied the breeder, walking back inside and laying Frank back on the floor. "That'll be a total of $1,200."

"Oof," said Jim, "that's quite a bit, but I think I can cover it, if I can see him again." He soon got out his credit card and swiped it over her phone's attached card reader. Once the payment went through and they said their goodbyes, Penangke grabbed a whining Frank and began stroking the puppy's back with his paw pads.

Jim and Penangke stepped out of the breeder's house as Jim asked, "So, uhh, how long did it take to remember yourself or whatever?"

"It took me about two years," said Penangke, "but every animal is different."

The End

13
SPACEFARERS

Six-hundred kilometers beyond the Earth's atmosphere, a lone American astronaut peacefully floated out of the airlock in the International Space Station with a toolbox in hand. He closed the square hatch and floated past a bank of laptops and various scientific equipment, piping equipment, and panels on the walls, floor, and ceiling.

Typing away at one of the laptops was a cosmonaut with light green skin and two sharp tusks as he labored away at a scientific paper and accompanying data sheets. Out the corner of his eye, he spotted the astronaut floating around inside the station.

"Ei, Brandon," he said in his best English. "What's the status on the telescope?"

"Well, Petya," replied Brandon, floating towards some metal brackets above the sleeping compartments, "the gamma ray burst monitor has begun to absorb too much radiation."

"Why don't I help you out of that suit, and we'll talk, alright?" asked Petya.

"Sounds great," said Brandon, latching himself on one of the on-board clamps and letting Petya take off his helmet. "So the telescope's motherboard has started to become irradiated and it's created a short in the data acquisition module."

"Jesus!" exclaimed Petya. "Why did you come back, that could be dangerous!"

"I know," said Brandon as the helmet was taken off, revealing an Elf with a square chin and deep brown eyebrows. "I turned it off, so it would stop absorbing all that radiation. I mean, it still has a half-life of 13 days, but at least it won't accelerate."

"Well, it sounds like we could be using magic to fix that," suggested Petya, his eyes growing wide as he slowly helped Brandon out of his suit.

"Maybe, but I don't see what kind of spell would help though," stated Brandon.

"Magic using makes you immune to the effects of radiation," explained Petya. "My dad worked in the Soviet nuclear program back in the day, and he told me that only the wizards were allowed to be in the fallout area without hazmat suits. They never got cancer or anything like that, so maybe there's a spell for binding neutrons out there."

"Great idea," said Brandon. "But, I don't know how well it works, I've never been into it."

"It wouldn't hurt to start," remarked Petya, "and now would be a perfect time to learn magic."

"But wouldn't my powers be too weak to alter something so…fundamental?" remarked Brandon, letting Petya detach the suit's jet pack. "And besides, I don't think we really brought any spell books up here."

"You can find spells on the internet," explained Petya. "It doesn't need to come out of a book to be magical."

"Wow," said Brandon with his eyes wide open. "I had no idea."

"Yeah," said Petya, "there's all kinds of spellcasting blogs where people upload different spells that, like have differing effects."

"Well, I might need to check them out sometime," said Brandon, letting go of his toolbox. "It would definitely save having to bring these tools through the airlock."

"I wouldn't say that," said Petya as the tools began to slowly float upwards, "unless you want to go back to school and become a Wizard."

"Oh, definitely not," chuckled Brandon. "But it would be nice if I could channel electricity through the grabbers."

"I'm sure it would," stated Petya, "but maybe now wouldn't be a good time. You've been working hard all day."

"Well, thank you," smiled Brandon. "Ever since I came here, I've wanted to help in whatever way I can."

"Yeah, you SpaceX guys are more useful than I thought," complemented Petya.

"Look, SpaceX might've sent us up here," explained Brandon, "but at the end of the day, I still work for NASA. So I'm a government drone like you."

"Oh, shut up," said Petya in an endearing tongue and cheek fashion.

Later, Brandon floated into a sleeping capsule just below the main module. There were no windows, but there were a couple sleeping bags and velcro straps to keep them from floating off. He crept into his sleeping bag and fastened it to the wall before he zipped it up and gradually went off to sleep.

When he awoke, he found himself in awe as he gazed up at a rather surreal purple and blue sky with ethereal trees sloping in and out of existence. White stars remained static while giant planets lay suspended in the sky as his sleeping bag was on a translucent whitish-blue force field that exposed churning magma beneath.

"Whoa," he said breathlessly, looking around as he reached for the zipper when his eyes widened once he noticed that he wasn't floating away. "G-gravity?!" he stammered. "What's going on!"

"Welcome to spirit heaven," said a mysterious voice.

Brandon looked around the strange place as the voice's words sunk like a poorly made cruise ship.

"Wait…heaven?!" he exclaimed before his face turned to dread. "Oh my God, am I dead?"

"Far from it," replied the voice as footsteps became closer until they crawled over toward Brandon and his sleeping bag. The creature in question was a hairless grizzly with well-manicured claws, soft, tanish-pale flesh, and a mouth of sharp teeth. Brandon was left speechless at such a bizarre creature as it reared on its hind legs and extended a paw towards him.

"Need some help up?" asked the creature.

"Oh," said Brandon, unzipping his sleeping bag and sliding out of it. He grabbed the creature's left paw and gradually got up with a struggle. "Man, I really need to spend time on the resistance machine," quipped Brandon as Uda went back down on his forelegs, and Brandon stared at the creature with awe and unsettling disgust. "Well, thanks, uhh…"

"Uda," said the creature. "You can call me Uda, the Bear Buddha. Don't be afraid of my shape. I'm here to guide your spirit as an enlightened teacher of supernature."

"Right," said Brandon as Uda began to walk away from the sleeping bag. "So if I'm not dead, then what the hell happened?"

"You're here because I saw you pondering spirituality and magic," said Uda. "I'm going to show you how to become enlightened."

"No, no, it's not that," replied Brandon, following the bear. "I'm not that into magic is all."

"You should know that magic and meditation is the way to everlasting life and liberation from suffering," said Uda with a smile. "You have a special gift."

"Well, that's nice and all," conceded Brandon. "But why live for millions of years just to stare out into the abyss?"

"Well," said Uda, "let me show you."

They walked over the translucent, smooth world as Brandon was left mesmerized by the churning and turning of the heavenly planet's mantle.

"So Uda, how long have you been doing this kind of teaching or whatever anyways?"

"For around 1,600 years now," explained Uda. "You'll see the other Buddhas soon enough."

They soon came upon the intricately made pipework that was the ISS. The chambers were all streaking red light towards them while Brandon look at the space station seemingly immobilized in time.

"Wait, is that what I think it is?" he asked.

"Indeed," replied Uda, reading the astronaut's mind. "Now, why don't we go in and see what we can see?" Uda phased through.

"Okay…" said Brandon apprehensively as he walked through the wall. Though as inquiring as he was, nothing could've prepared him for what he saw. "Woah!" he said. "I can't believe this!" What he saw were the deep, see-through green souls resting inside vaguely human shaped spirits of his fellow astronauts. "Amazing," said Brandon, inspecting one of the souls to find a dream playing like a video on a phone screen.

"Yes, travelling at 20 times faster than sound and yet they're resting peacefully in midair," admired Uda. "You Earthlings have surely come a long way. Not even the first Buddha would've even dreamed of man doing something like this."

Brandon inspected the dream as it came into focus. He saw a yeti made of rice up to its navel in the waters of a rice farm.

The yeti looked down upon the astronaut as he appeared to be navigating the rice plants like a maze with stoic determination on his face.

"This is Ozaki's dream," stated Brandon.

"Indeed," replied Uda. "When the soul isn't used, it taps into the basest parts of ourselves both in mind and spirit. Only a natural telepath would be able to see this."

"What do you mean?" asked Brandon. "People don't see each other's dreams like this? I thought it was normal."

"Far from it. Only witches, Wizards, and spirits can see this in normal circumstances," explained Uda. "Right now, you're seeing the truest self as its held within the body is the mark of a psychic. Through the meditative practice, you will have a chance to unlock this power and attain everlasting bliss within a few lifetimes. Since there's no sound in space, you can start meditating easily without gravity keeping you down."

Brandon stroked his chin and mulled it over a bit.

"Y'know what," he said. "Maybe I will." Then at that moment, everything began to turn black, and Brandon began to panic. "Hey Uda, what's going on?"

"Oh no! It's y—"

And soon there was silence as dark blue filled his view until he stood in the middle of an abandoned city with overgrown buildings and manors. The ISS would seem frozen in time as the blue marble known as Earth was plainly visible beneath his feet. There was also an Angel flying around the broken metallic mansions with dark red and gray wings and a deep blue business suit as if studying a lost relic.

He flew down towards Brandon, gently landing in front of him.

"Hello Brandon," he said with a sly yet pompous grin.

"Who are you?" he asked. "What the hell is going on now?"

"I'm your Guardian Angel, Te-meok," explained the Angel "I was assigned your case on January 14th 1999, at 11:34 AM Mountain Standard Time"

"What do you mean?" asked Brandon.

"Sir, I can understand your confusion," consoled Te-meok, "but, I have your baptism entry here, and the numbers don't lie." He held it up, showing the divine piece of paperwork with a picture of an eight year old Brandon getting baptized in a swimming pool of holy water clipped onto the document's top right.

"Yeah, I was a baptized Mormon," said Brandon, recalling painful childhood memories of parental control and sexual repression. "So what?"

"So, by baptism in the Church of Jesus Christ of Latter Day Saints followed by a Confirmation," explained the Angel "you have received the gift of God and signed a very important contract with the good Lord." He pointed upwards, motioning to God.

"And then I grew up and saw sense," pouted Brandon. "Can't a man just be free!"

"When you're consorting with Satan, you can't!" said the Angel. "I'm here to protect you and deliver you from evil. I mean, other than this space stuff, your life must surely be quite hollow and empty without God."

"What are you talking about? I have a lovely wife back on Earth, and we've been married for five years now!" said Brandon. "Besides, why would I put my faith in a God that leaves people in the darkness for all eternity?"

"Age of accountability," said the Angel in a sing-songy voice. "You'd have been mature enough to make those kinds of decisions."

"I was just a kid then," complained Brandon. "I mean, you wouldn't give an eight-year-old a gun or let him vote."

"No, but we're not talking about that now," said Te-meok. "Let me show you something." He soon turned around and motioned Brandon to follow. He looked at the corroded and rusting mansions, rotting decrepit malls, and ethereal streets.

"This was the city of Achtmorgen," explained Te-meok. "In the precontact days, I was just a mortal in the Ute tribe of Angels until deities made me one of their own, and I was made to do landscaping here, blew my mind that we even could command plants like that in the hunter-gatherer days."

"But what happened?" asked Brandon, looking around at the ruins.

"God merely set everything right by gradually revealing aspects of his infinity over the span of millennia, and phased greedy, exploitative deities out of power," explained Te-meok. "God is the most supreme of all, for He's all knowing, all seeing, and all present. He's infinite in size and power. He knows about every little sin and act of good in your life. He had a plan for you that he made back in the nineties."

"And let me guess, all this weird stuff wouldn't be happening if I were wearing my magical underpants?" said Brandon, rolling his eyes.

"First of all, it's a temple garment," said Te-meok angrily. "And second, temptation produces greed, which produces suffering for all your fellow man. So why suffer all those lifetimes of temptation when there's a world of eternal happiness waiting for you?"

He soon woke up in his sleeping bag, wondering if the whole thing was a dream.

Later that morning, they had rehydrated and microwaved miso soup, egg, and salmon out of the microwave panel.

"This tastes good," remarked one of the astronauts. "We never get to have stuff like this back in Russia," said Petya.

"Thanks," said Ozaki in his best English. "The JAXA have always been great with their rations."

"Mind if I ask you something?" said Brandon.

"Of course," replied Ozaki.

"So I had these weird dreams where I was in heaven, and this weird hairless bear monster showed me all your dreams and lectured me about religion and crap," explained Brandon

"Ah, that's a Buddha Kami," explained Ozaki. "They're divine beings or manifestations of nature in the Shinto pantheon. They work as divine teachers of philosophy."

"And guardian Angels?" asked Brandon coldly.

"Not normally. They don't bother with western guardian spirits," replied Ozaki. "But what's this stuff about dreams?"

"Like, I see other people's dreams and stuff," said Brandon with a tone of confusion "You mean all of you don't?"

"Not really, no," explained Petya frankly. "That's something special with you."

"Is it really that profound that I can see dreams?" said Brandon in disbelief.

One of the American astronauts nearly did a spit take before swallowing her blob of water.

"Sorry, it's just funny that you've had these powers and just…never thought about them."

"I mean, the temple would always go on about how we get personal revelation from God" explained Brandon as Te-meok joined them in spirit standing on the floor as if there were gravity on the space station "I just always assumed that these revelations would come in my sleep."

"Personal revelations?" asked Petya "Do those mormon guys think every one of their followers is a damn Priest or something?"

"Hey, my folks were very religious," said Brandon as Te-meok looked down at him, pouting. "They would've flipped if they saw me with a bear spirit!"

Later, astronauts could be seen huddling around the telescope with Geiger counters in tow. It had been long been powered off.

"Holy hell!" exclaimed the astronaut, looking down at the Geiger counter. "The radiation levels are off the charts. Are you sure you turned it off, Brandon?"

"Yeah," replied Brandon as the Geiger counter was silent in the vacuum of space. "I was out here yesterday, so I don't really know why there's all this cosmic radiation."

"I was there to help you out of your suit when I advised you did magic," explained Petya as a reflective patch slimed away from the telescope. The astronauts would continue talking as the metallic blob floated upwards, pulsing its body like an octopus until it began to float towards an astronaut's jetpack. It expanded over the jetpack and then to the helmet, as the other astronauts could now plainly see liquid metal seemingly consuming her alive.

"Hey! Tina!" explained Brandon. "There's weird shit on your head!"

But before she could do anything else, the puddle grew sharp spikes that punctured a great gaping hole in the front of her helmet. The metallic being let go and began to change shape into a form that was vaguely Human like—with arms, legs, and a head.

"Holy shit!" exclaimed Brandon as the astronaut's face was sucked toward the end of the helmet, and blood, carbon dioxide, and oxygen spewed out into the vacuum of space.

They liquified into a blue, bubbling haze that flowed out of the hole while the astronaut's blood boiled, and her eyes bulged from her sockets. She gasped for air before screaming in pain as blood stained her suit, and the others frantically jetted towards the suit's oxygen supply. The being soon formed a forcefield, bouncing them all back toward the space station.

Boiling blood streamed out of her body a while large portions of her skin, muscles, bones, and organs were soon ripped from her body by the intense force of the vacuum. A foreign thought entered Brandon's mind as he turned his jetpack on: *Return to spirituality or die with your colleagues.* Strange hairless creatures began to come out of a portal only Brandon could see.

"I don't know what's going on, but you guys can't be out here!" he exclaimed

The others had quickly begun to jet towards the airlock with their jetpacks as Angels grabbed onto the cosmonauts while the hairless Buddhas wrapped their hooves and paws around the astronauts.

The master needs humans to be stupid, thought the being. Brandon was drawn towards the portal though he was trying to go to the airlock. *Your probes violate the master's privacy, and Humans are too stupid and narrow-minded to control spirituality.*

"Brandon, where the hell are you going?" asked Petya, turning down towards them.

"You don't see it?!" exclaimed Brandon. "There's like this black hole portal that's sucking me in!"

"This guy has gone crazy," complained a cosmonaut in Russian. "Let's help him. That thing must've gotten to him!"

"I'm not crazies!" exclaimed Brandon in broken Russian as he was still being drawn backwards toward the portal. "There's Angels and Kami all over you! You crazies cannot view it!"

"What the hell are you talking about, Brandon?" asked Petya. "There's nothing like that out here. Now get back in here before that thing kills you!"

Before Brandon could respond, he had seemingly disappeared into thin air. Petya gasped and asked in English,

"Brandon?" but there was no reply on the suit's radio. "Brandon, do you copy?" Again, there was nothing but silence as the metallic being went into the invisible portal, leaving the corpse behind in orbit.

Brandon was ejected out to spirit heaven, where he was surrounded by a forest of redwood trees and constellations of planets in the drab green sky. His helmet was scratched and dented up on tree bark. Uda and Te-meok stood on opposite sides of Brandon, separated by a group of people in varying eras of historical attire. He disabled oxygen and carbon dioxide before taking off his helmet and getting up. His brows were scrunched, and his face was as red as a sunburn.

"That is a specialist piece of equipment!" he said, wiping dirt off the legs of the suit. "You better explain what's going on here, or I'm gonna kick your ass where the sun don't shine."

"Your probes and telescopes violate our privacy," explained Uda. "Tabloids of the heavenly plane got pictures of our bedrooms."

"If that's all it was, you wouldn't send me here when there's a freaky monster killing us all!" exclaimed Brandon as the being came through the portal before hitting a tree.

"I paid off the speculus to sabotage your little telescope," said Te-meok with a snicker as Brandon stared at the being's head, only to see his face in the reflection.

"Wait, that thing is a speculus!" exclaimed Brandon, pointing at the being as his reflection showed his head shrinking.

You need to brush up on your demonology, telepathized the speculus. *You should know that our kind commands caesnium, for it is what makes us tick.*

"That has gamma rays!" exclaimed Brandon before turning towards Te-meok. "So what the hell is going on, and why are there all these people here?"

"These," said Uda, "are some of your ancestors going back ten generations."

"We just figured you needed to hear the wisdom from your elders," stated Te-meok. "Elders have life experience that makes them wise and respected."

"We're quite ashamed of you!" pouted a dress wearing ancestor in Greek. "Your wiccan ways are a disgrace!"

"Magic is just as much a part of nature as bunny rabbits!" exclaimed Brandon as a look of surprise came over his face. "Wait, how can I understand you?"

"You don't have to try using your powers here," said an ancestor with a long beard. "You're outside of your physical plane here; you've transcended beyond the maladies of your body."

"Hiram, that's a load of baloney!" bickered Brandon's great grandad. "God blessed him, endowing him with the gift of tongues. He's merely speaking in tongues."

"Look, look," said Brandon in an attempt to calm the two down. "Whatever is going on, you surely must know how to deal with these invasive spirits."

"Methinks you oughta pick the Angel" said an ancestor with a northern English accent. "God's got 'is fiery bow pointed down to you!"

"Honestly, I don't see what the problem is," shrugged Hiram. "Just choose neither and let these two rascals face divine justice in hell if they killed a man."

"Woman, but the point still stands," said Brandon.

"It's immoral and sinful to consort with a fallen Angel," said another Greek ancestor. "Just let the oriental spirits guide you; you won't be executed for it."

"But just because you can doesn't mean you should," said a Norwegian ancestor. "The bear monster is an abomination and an agent of Satan!"

"Please return to Mormonism," begged Te-meok. "You will be happier and humbler, like your days as a missionary."

"Mormonism!" exclaimed Hiram. "You were in that crazy cult!"

"Y-yeah," said Brandon. "I was born into it."

"Well, leave them all behind!" boomed Hiram. "I reckon they're a bunch of queer suppressive whack jobs. You have self-determination. You're better than these race cultists!"

"Those American cults are shameful!" exclaimed a German ancestor. "I think the bear is kinda weird, but at least he's concerned about your mind and how you're doing."

"Don't mess with me!" exclaimed Te-meok. "You don't want to see my higher form!"

Uda, Brandon, and the ancestors all looked at Te-meok dumbfounded as he began to grow in size. His arms turned to wings that slid down the sides of his body. His normal wings started to slowly sprout eyes along with his legs. His toes merged together into one nailless digit, which too would grow eyelashes, eyelids, and finally, a network of eyes.

The eyes on his head began to shrink as his suit dissolved into the aether, revealing that Te-meok's chest and stomach had grown eyes as well. Three other heads grew: one was the head of a cougar; the other, the head of a great buck; and the rearmost was that of a vulture.

"You'll regret this, Brandon," said all four heads at once. "God Almighty will now commence smiting!" And in the blink of an eye, Te-meok took flight, and other monstrous Angels appeared with angered eyes on seemingly every possible body part. Uda soon began to chant a portal into existence while the ancestors made a run for it. Through the portal came Buddha Kamis as hairless monkeys rode hairless horses, and alligators had mounted featherless ostriches, each of them with pistols and submachine guns in hand.

"You abominations are clouding this man's mind!" exclaimed Uda. "You will pay for leaking my e-mail to the heavenly guard!"

The two sides began shooting each other with bullets, and eye lasers were being fired back and forth. Brandon backed away from the gun fight and ran away before Te-meok's vulture head cast a forcefield on the battlefield, keeping him from going anywhere.

The Buddhas opened fire on the Angels with bullets spewing from the bushes, the leaves, and the ground. The Angels, meanwhile, warped and teleported all over the forest; not even two bullets in the chest eye would stop them.

"Slay any goddamn devil you see!" commanded the Dominion Angels with two of their heads talking at once. "I want these abominations stuffed as trophies!"

"Yes, sir!" saluted the Archangels before flying over towards where featherless hawks had been perched with their sniper rifles. One bullet vanquished an angel back to the highest of heavens, while another angel fired a beam of dark magic, instantly vaporizing two birds.

"Brandon!" exclaimed a familiar voice as footsteps ran up towards him as he was cowering.

"Petya!" said Brandon, seeing him with couple guns in hand.

"They're planning an offensive on the ISS to capture our intel!"

"What the hell?!" exclaimed Brandon. "How did you get here, and why are you acting so strange?"

"I made a portal to get here!" exclaimed Petya. "And I was drafted into a tour of Chechnya before becoming an astronaut. Follow my lead!"

Brandon nodded and ran after him. The two shot down Buddhas and Angels alike as a blue outline of the ISS had come nearer and nearer. Brandon shot an Archangel in the back eye before she had the chance to fire an eye beam.

It was just then that a hairless fox charged out of the bushes, and Brandon proceeded to kick it into the line of fire. The two ran in and around the trees only for an Angel to cast a fire spell on their jetpacks, which soon blew up in two massive, orange, fiery explosions, setting the trees ablaze and burning their backs.

They would be dead if time hadn't stopped, and a strange force healed their wounds and dispelled the fire. Time resumed as Brandon and Petya were launched off their feet before sliding across the ground, screaming. The Angels stopped pursuing them as looks of horror sat on each of their ghoulish faces.

"Oh," Brandon grunted in pain while Petya, being an Ork was unphased by the impact, but had a rather puzzled look on his face.

"What the hell happened to the fire?" asked Petya as a mysterious and powerful voice spoke up.

"I liberated you, my child."

A white helicopter could be seen floating overhead, it's rotors not spinning, creating a cross-shaped shadow on the ground.

"Please, Your Holiness," said Te-meok out of his deer head, bowing before the helicopter. It was just then that a nude, hairless Human with no apparent genitals faded into existence from nothing. "We were just trying to expose the depraved Satanic morals of the Buddhas"

"As head teacher and guide of the Buddhas, I have no part in this," said the man humbly. "What these Buddhas did were depraved and are a disgrace to the philosophy of enlightenment!"

"Who the heck are you two?" asked Brandon.

"You may call me the Holy Spirit," said the helicopter. "I'm a sort of puppet of God, so He can show Himself to the finite folk."

"And I'm Gautama Buddha," said the man, "head of the Buddhist religion and teacher to the Gods."

"But if that is the Holy Spirit," said Brandon confused, "why isn't he Human?"

"I can be," said God, morphing into a pale, dark-haired human. "I can be anything. The Mormon church taught you wrong." God soon turned towards his Angels "They might've been stealing credit card numbers, but that's no excuse to cause all of this trouble."

"Wait," said Brandon. "All this over a some stupid credit cards!"

"We needed to keep them from sending them over to their associates on the dwarf planets," explained Te-meok. "If we hadn't sabotaged the telescope, more people might've gotten robbed!"

"I am especially ashamed of you, Uda" said Siddhartha. "It is our duty to teach the worldly the ways of enlightenment, but this violates at least five of the ten precepts for Buddhas!"

"Your Eminence, I do apologize," said Uda, kneeling before Siddhartha. Siddhartha teleported them far away from the spirit heaven as God vanished along with all the Angels.

"I've never known God to do shit like this," said Petya as the telescope glided and phased through the trees at a slow, but steady pace.

"Yeah," said Brandon. "The Lord works in strange ways."

The End

EPILOGUE

The world is a very complicated place to live in and people spend their entire lifetimes trying to make sense of it all. Anything that brings us comfort seemingly has some form of vice or propaganda attached to it while virtuous truth gets frowned upon either because it's too boring or lacks a straight forward right and wrong. The last three years were living proof of this mental power struggle between the factual science and the emotional spirituality.

We aren't cloistered hermit crabs or a hive of bees and we're not exactly logical objective machines or carnal instinct-driven animals. Complications in life start when we realize that we're massively varied collections of individuals. It's the social structure our prehistoric ancestors chose in a world of death, tragedy and suffering,

It's maddening to apply black and white thinking to a world so random in its distribution of moral systems and personal hardship. There aren't any super powerful villains who out-evil one-another the way we were shown by culture, adages, religion and popular media. Perhaps for simplicity, we were told that whatever is taboo is bad and anything that seems easier on people's ears are good.

Yet, if you think of some of the worst atrocities or the most gruesome crimes committed in human history, they were done by people who saw their horrible deeds as the noblest thing they could possibly do. Some might call them sick, twisted, deluded, stupid or even evil. But it all ignores the fact that they saw themselves as the hero who felt compelled to commit atrocities and human rights violations in order to thwart the efforts of the villain.

As much as this realization was a tough pill for me to swallow, the world began making so much more sense. In a lot of ways, we're hardwired to think in terms of heroes and villains while knowledge comes off as boring noise due to its inability to tell a good story about people who do what they believe is right. It gives us wonderful inventions and terms, but its nonstop string of Greco-Roman Pidgin English and data sheets fail to engage with people who aren't confrontational geeks or academics.

This effects our imagination as well since tropes stem from the attitudes, opinions and social customs of people that surrounded the times of the original creator as shortcuts to help with writer's block at best and convince someone to kill at worst. For this reason anything fantastical was heavily segregated from anything resembling science to the point where science fantasy media is thought of as outright science-fiction.

Similiar to the way we compartmentalize religion and science, we kept genre fiction well separated into two strict boxes: The fringe/medieval box and the future box. These boxes have strict boundaries heavily guarded by the paratroopers known as sensibility. It took until the advent of video games, a medium that wasn't strictly reliant on a story and plot, to override the usual anxieties and inhibitions to try new things in the fantasy genre.

Though my work is offbeat and odd, I did it for the same reason Homer and the Brothers Grimm did it: To make sense of a confusing world by inserting wild imagination and whimsy into a cold uncaring universe. Knowledge hasn't had a decent narrator in over a hundred years and religions haven't addressed the facts of the here now in well over a century. We just got so lost in the fairy tales of knights, Princesses and horrible monsters that we've forgotten about the magic present in our incredible World of Legends.